MAN IN DUPLICATE

Playboy millionaire Harvey Bradman is set an ultimatum by his fiancée: before she marries him, he must carry out some significant, courageous act. Amazingly, the next day the newspaper carries a full report of Harvey's heroic rescue of a woman from her stalled car on a level crossing, avoiding a rail crash! But Harvey had been asleep in bed at the time of the incident. And when his mysterious twin seeks him out, he becomes enmeshed in a sinister conspiracy . . .

JOHN RUSSELL FEARN

MAN IN DUPLICATE

Complete and Unabridged

LINFORD
Leicester

First published in Great Britain

First Linford Edition
published 2007

British Library CIP Data

Fearn, John Russell, *1908 – 1960*
  Man in duplicate.—Large print ed.—
Linford mystery library
  1. Detective and mystery stories
  2. Large type books
  I. Title II. Statten, Vargo
823.9′12 [F]

ISBN 978–1–84617–948–8

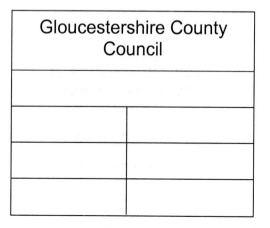

Gloucestershire County Council

1

Unlikely hero

The two had been at the secluded corner table of the exclusive nightspot for over an hour. Their conversation had been so engrossing they had failed to notice the cabaret show, furthermore, they had not risen to take part in the general floor dancing, which was unusual, since the couple were known to be two of the best dancers in London's upper social set.

The girl was looking serious and determined. She was attired in the very latest evening gown and the gems that flashed at intervals from her ears and wrists were genuine. She was black-haired, creamy-skinned, and as good looking as cosmetics could make her.

Her escort, and donor of the jewelry, was immaculate in the male fashion, the silk revers on his evening jacket occasionally catching the light. Blond, good-looking, worth several millions, Harvey Bradman was quite the most eligible playboy bachelor in town. Even so, and despite the fact that she knew many rivals might leap into the gap she was making, Vera Maynard was absolute in her refusal to marry him. Hence the absorption: hence Harvey's pleadings.

'Can't see the reason,' he said at last, with a moody glance around him. 'I hope I'm a hundred per cent male, and it certainly can't be that I haven't enough money to look after you, unless there's some kind of parental opposition? No, even that isn't possible. You're of age and can please yourself. So what is it?'

Vera gave a faint smile. 'Just can't guess it, can you? You've waltzed around everything and never seen the reason for my turning down your proposal.'

Harvey pondered, genuinely worried. Vera did not interrupt him. She sipped her wine and waited.

'Can only be you just plain don't like me,' Harvey sighed at last. 'Which is an awful pity. I'd sort of got the idea in the few months we've known each other that we — '

'Oh, I like you enough, Harvey.'

'Can't do, or you'd agree to marry me.'

'I will when you make yourself worthwhile.'

Harvey's expression changed and his blue eyes studied the girl's face. 'Make myself worthwhile? So that's it! You think I'm a waster!'

'I know you are. I don't mean that nastily, believe me.' Vera's hand rested upon his. 'You're one of the best fellows in the world, and as generous a man as one could wish to meet — but you definitely are throwing your life away. Just because your father made several millions as a shipping line magnate is no reason for you to drift around doing nothing.'

'Become one of the common herd, eh?' Harvey grinned. 'Take the 'bus to work every morning and get my meals in a downtown café at cut rates?'

'That would hardly be necessary, though I don't suppose it would do you any harm.' Vera released his hand and sat back in her chair. 'No, the kind of thing I envisage is you at the top of some particular profession — say architecture, engineering, chemistry, or something like that. Choose whichever you prefer and make a good job of it.'

'At twenty-eight!' Harvey gasped. 'Dammit, Vera, I'm an old man!'

'Not too old to learn. Plenty of great men didn't start anything vital until they reached thirty. You can do the same.'

'And am I to assume that during this — er — apprenticeship you would calmly sit around and wait for me? With the kind of mind I've got I'd probably be sixty before I drew my first pay.'

'I'd wait — and don't exaggerate!' Vera added severely. 'You are quite capable enough only you don't try. Can't you see that it is because I'm fond of you that I want you to make something of your life?'

'Make the world a better place for having been here, eh?' Harvey was still grinning. 'You're the most frightful optimist, Vee, and a bit crazy too. Here am I with millions, a town and country house, and all the outpourings of my generous heart — and you want me to become a council house builder, or something.'

'I didn't say that. Stick to the point. I work too, you know, even though dad has more money than he'll ever use. I'm head of the Women's Help Legion.'

'Oh,' Harvey said solemnly; then his mood changed abruptly. 'Oh, chuck all this rot, Vee! It doesn't make sense in our set — '

'It does to me. If you find you can't make a career in time, then do something noteworthy. One act to get out of yourself and prove you're capable of standing on your own two feet.'

Harvey got up deliberately. 'Time I took you home, Vee. You're getting light-headed.'

'Not a bit of it. I've given you the conditions on which I'll marry you. It's up to you now. I'll certainly never tie myself to a playboy with nothing to recommend him but his bank balance.' Vera gently pushed away the chinchilla cape, which Harvey held ready for her. 'I'm not going home yet, Harvey. I'm expecting Maisie to drop in and I want a word with her.'

Harvey sighed and lowered the cape to the chair back again. 'Then, Miss Maynard, if I have your permission I will withdraw, if only to give your proposition some thought. May I disturb you on the 'phone in the morning about mid-day?'

'You may.'

Harvey stooped, kissed her smooth forehead somewhat perfunctorily, and then wandered from the opulent dining room. He gathered his hat and coat from the cloakroom and drifted out of the nightspot in something of a daze.

'Your car, Mr. Bradman?' the commissionaire asked.

'Car? Eh — oh, yes . . . Look, Charles,' Harvey continued, as the commissionaire gave a signal, 'what would you call a very courageous act?'

Charles looked vaguely surprised, but he was accustomed to handling all kinds of customers.

'I'd say going to the dentist, sir, and telling him to take out every tooth without gas!'

Harvey sighed. 'That wouldn't convince her. Thanks all the same. Here, buy yourself a couple of cigars.'

'Thank you, sir.' Charles pocketed the money, held open the rear door of the limousine, and then closed it again as Harvey sank wearily into the cushions.

'Home, Richards,' he told the chauffeur. 'Miss Maynard will not be with me tonight.'

'Very good, Mr. Bradman.'

Harvey remained in his abstracted mood all the way to his town residence just off Piccadilly Circus. He was still looking profoundly sorry for himself as Peters, his manservant, relieved him of his hat and coat.

'Are we not feeling very well, sir?' Peters asked.

'I'm fine,' Harvey replied solemnly.

Peters knew better than to argue but he could be permitted the doubt on his lean face. He was a tall man in the late fifties, punctual as the sunrise and extremely devoted to the drifting young man who, he secretly felt — as Vera Maynard did — had hidden possibilities.

'My apologies, sir, but I have not yet had supper prepared for you. You are, if I may say so, a trifle early.'

'Two hours early,' Harvey agreed. 'I've had what is known in vulgar parlance as the brush-off.'

'Indeed, sir?' Peters glided to the massive mahogany hall wardrobe, rid himself of the hat and coat, closed cellophane wrappers over them, and then returned to Harvey's side.

'Am I to assume that Miss Maynard was responsible, sir?'

'The assumption is correct. Come and fix me a 'scarlet lady', Peters, and I'll tell you all about it. I think you may be able to help me.'

'I'd be delighted, sir.'

Peters paced majestically behind Harvey as he wandered into the lounge and threw himself on the divan. Then he found his drink beside him on the occasional table. He looked up at Peter's waiting figure.

'Peters, I have either to decide on a career, and finish at the head of it, or else I have to perform an act which will make everybody realize I don't exclusively spend my time getting rid of money and filling myself with drink.'

Peters gave a faint, impersonal smile. 'The terms of Miss Maynard before she will marry you, sir?'

'How did you guess?' Harvey moodily sipped his drink.

'Well, sir, you did mention before departing this evening that you were — hmm — going to 'pop the question' to Miss Maynard, so my deduction is hardly brilliant.'

Harvey finished his drink, then got to his feet.

'Point is, Peters, what in blazes am I going to do? I can't start learning a profession at my age. Besides, there isn't any profession I'm interested in.'

'You have at times evinced an interest in things scientific, sir. You certainly have a profound interest in the present day tendencies of science.'

'I know, but that's purely what any intelligent person would have. It doesn't say I should work myself into a second Einstein, or something, does it?'

Since Peters frankly considered this an impossibility he passed no comment.

'Some brave deed.' Harvey stood

musing. 'Happen to know any blondes who want carrying out of a burning building, Peters?'

'Even if I did I would suggest that such a matter would be safer in the hands of the fire brigade, sir. In fact, thinking the matter over, it would appear that Miss Maynard has posed quite a difficult proposition.'

'Difficult! It's monstrous!'

Peters waited, his upward turned eyes revealing the profundity of his concentration.

'Maybe I'll think better in the morning,' Harvey said at length, shrugging. 'For once in my wild, mad life I'll turn in early.'

'Very good, sir.'

And so, by one o'clock Harvey was fast asleep, and to judge from the smile on his face Vera's ultimatum was not troubling him very deeply. Peters for his part tried to think of something original and within the range of his young master's capabilities — but at last he decided he could not make bricks without straw and so also went to sleep.

At seven o'clock he was astir as usual to prepare Harvey's early cup of tea. This was the time of day that Peters liked. He was the sole servant in the house and when Harvey was not around Peters became a human being, smoked at his work, and never wore his jacket.

He collected the paper from the front doormat and took it into the kitchen to enjoy a cup of tea and read the news. Then his eye presently lighted on a photograph and he gave a violent start and the half filled teacup dropped unheeded to the floor.

'Blow me down!' Peters exclaimed blankly.

Still regardless of the fallen teacup he gazed at that photograph of Harvey — for there was no doubt but that it was Harvey — and then his eye traveled to the single word over the top of the photo. It said — HERO!

Peters, still looking petrified, lowered his gaze to the column below the picture and read it quickly: then he read again more deliberately, struggling to assimilate the impossible.

Last night, close to midnight, Miss Janet Thompson, a newspaper correspondent, was suddenly taken ill in her car. Out of control, it plunged through the Upper Namos level crossing gates and came to a standstill on the railway line.

Mrs. Cardwell, controller of the gates — one of the few women level-crossing keepers in the country — failed in her efforts to drag the unconscious woman free so hurried to signal an oncoming train to stop.

Whilst she was making her preparations a man came upon the scene, lifted Miss Thompson clear of the car, and then with unusual strength dragged the vehicle back from the line, thereby preventing what might otherwise have been a serious accident to the train.

The unknown rescuer corrected the defect in the car engine caused by the impact with the crossing gates and drove Miss Thompson to the nearest doctor. She soon recovered consciousness and was entirely unaware

of her narrow escape until her benefactor explained the circumstances in
which he had found her. She insisted
that his bravery be made public and
his photograph be taken — which
this newspaper is only too willing to
do. Miss Thompson will be remembered for her interesting articles on
the fashion page.

The rescuer refused to give his
name and, after the photograph had
been taken, quietly slipped away.

'I'll be triple damned!' declared Peters
frankly, his gaze back on the photograph
again. 'That it is His Nibs is beyond
doubt — but how the devil did he do it?
Upper Namos? Where in blazes is that?'

Peters thought for a moment, then he
got to his feet and went into the small but
well stocked library. A search through a
Gazetteer revealed that Upper Namos
was some twenty miles away on the north
side of London.

'Couldn't be,' Peters muttered blankly.
'It just isn't possible. And anyway His
Nibs wouldn't, unless he sleep-walks,

which to the best of my knowledge he doesn't.'

Conjectures having exhausted themselves Peters prepared Harvey's cup of tea and then took it in to him. He entered the bedroom with some trepidation as though he expected to find Harvey pacing up and down the room declaring his heroism. But no such phenomenon was present. Harvey was buried deeply under the bedclothes and, as usual, only stirred at the third shake on the shoulder.

'Morning already?' he growled at last, pushing his tousled head into view. 'Seven thirty?'

'Seven thirty, sir, yes.' Peters was gazing fixedly, the folded morning paper under his arm.

'Humph,' Harvey grunted, or something like it, and took the teacup. 'We'll have to adjust these early hours, Peters. Seven-thirty is a disgusting hour to be aroused for the purpose of drinking tea.'

'Just so, sir. Er — if you will forgive the question, sir, have you been anywhere during the night?'

Harvey peered through his tousled

blond hair. 'Been anywhere? What on earth are you talking about? Why should I go anywhere when I've a perfectly good bed to stop in?'

'No reason, sir, only it happens that something is puzzling me a great deal. Briefly — this!' Peters held forth the paper dramatically.

Harvey was stupidly sleepy and could hardly see the print — but he could certainly see his own photograph and the effect upon him was to make him drop the remains of his tea over the eiderdown. Instantly Peters fled for the necessities to remove the defilement and by the time he had finished his mopping up operations Harvey had read the column. His mouth was wide open and his eyes vacant.

'I'm still asleep,' he said finally. 'That's the answer.'

'On the contrary, sir, you are irrevocably awake.' Peters placed a soaking rag on the tray. 'That column actually does exist and that is your photograph.'

'So — so it would seem.' Harvey swallowed something. 'This is too much to spring on a man at this hour in the morning! What's the explanation, do you suppose?'

'I was hoping, sir, that you would be able to provide it. That is why I asked if you had been anywhere during the night. You retired early last night, twenty to twelve to be exact, and then presumably fell asleep — '

'Towards one,' Harvey put in, hugging his knees. 'Until then I couldn't get Vee off my mind. All this business with the fainting reporter happened around midnight at a distance of about — how the hell far is Upper Thingummybob?'

'After a rough estimate, sir, about twenty miles.' Peters did not add he had just consulted the Gazetteer: he preferred to sound knowledgeable.

'Twenty miles? Oh, this is idiotic! Must be somebody very like me — identical in fact. After all, everybody is supposed to have a double and this chap is mine. Might even be a distant relation. Didn't give his name, unfortunately.'

'I would be more inclined to say fortunately, sir.'

Harvey was quite awake by now. 'Fortunately? How come?'

'Well, sir, last night we were wrestling with Miss Maynard's ultimatum. One brave deed was all she asked of you. From the look of this she's got it — added to your profound modesty in refusing to reveal your name. Even the caption over the photo says 'Hero!' A tailor-made job, sir, if you ask me.'

Harvey was silent for a moment, thinking. Then: 'And what happens if this other blighter shows up?'

'Shows up where, sir?'

'Well, I — er — That is — ' Harvey pushed the hair out of his eyes. 'I see your point. I let Vee think that I did this job. And the only thing that can ever make her know otherwise is her meeting the actual fellow who'll let the cat out of the bag.'

'Just so, sir, which I think we can relegate to the highly improbable. Further, if he is as modest as he appears to be, he will never speak of his act of gallantry. Whether this story is covered by other newspapers we do not know, but I would consider it most unlikely. In fact no such splurge would have been made at all had not this young woman been a correspondent of that paper. In any event, Miss Maynard must certainly see this.'

'Right!' Harvey agreed, rubbing his hands. 'In fact, manna from heaven, Peters. I don't know how it happened, or who this benefactor is, but I raise my hat to him.' Harvey became silent and he frowned. Peters waited in calm silence.

'It's a mystery,' Harvey confessed presently. 'I mean, that this chap should be so like me. I haven't a twin brother or anybody with a striking resemblance to me. Just wonder who he is?'

'Hardly relevant, sir. Shall I hand you the telephone?'

Harvey nodded absently, but just as Peters had placed his hand on the extension instrument it rang stridently. Peters raised the 'phone to his ear.

'The Bradman residence. Oh, good morning, Miss Maynard.' Peters exchanged a look with Harvey. 'Yes, he is awake. I will connect you if you will please wait a moment.'

Harvey took the 'phone and Peters put a hand over the mouthpiece.

'Remember, sir, to boost this for all you're worth — if that is Miss Maynard's reason for ringing you, as I imagine it must be.'

Harvey grinned and cleared his throat. 'Hello, darling! Why this? Didn't I say I'd ring you around noon?'

'Noon won't do, Harvey. I've got to have the answer to this one immediately! What exactly did you do at the Upper Namos level-crossing last night? You're on the front page of the *News* in case you don't know.'

'I was afraid of that,' Harvey sighed. 'As for the incident itself, it was nothing.'

'On the contrary it sounds very courageous. The only thing puzzling me is where you got your strength from.'

'My strength?'

'Certainly! Fancy you pushing a car from a level crossing! It's tough enough to push a car at any time, and from the bumps in a level crossing it's murder. You're a lot stronger than I ever imagined.'

Harvey laughed airily. 'There's a lot of things about me which you don't know anything about, darling. Anyway, I hope you're satisfied. You wanted me to be a hero: well, there it is. Much quicker than swotting up on a new career or something like that.'

'Darling, I'm proud of you!' came Vera's ecstatic voice. 'It's only one act you've performed, but I'll keep to my side of the bargain and accept your proposal. When do we meet so you can give me the engagement ring?'

'Do you have to be so business-like about it?' Harvey complained. 'However, since you ask: how about my taking you out to lunch?'

'Done! Noon sharp I'll expect you.'

'It shall be done,' Harvey promised solemnly, and rang off. Peters took the telephone from him and then rubbed his palms softly together.

'I gather, sir, that Miss Maynard is convinced?'

'Absolutely! Makes it all the better that she read the thing herself without prompting. The grey pin-stripe, Peters! I have things to do.'

And, at exactly noon, Harvey's enormous sports car with himself at the wheel drew up outside the exclusive block of flats wherein Vera Maynard lived, moved, and had her being.

Humming to himself, impeccably dressed, Harvey stepped to the pavement — and then he hesitated. A man was watching him from a fair distance. Not that there was anything so dramatic about this: the queer part lay in the fact that Harvey realized immediately he was looking at an exact double of himself, though not in similar clothes.

'I'll be hanged,' Harvey murmured; then he suddenly beckoned quickly and took a stride forward. Far from obeying the summons the man took to his heels and started running — and it was quite the fastest run Harvey had ever seen. He gave it up after covering half a dozen yards in pursuit — then noting that the road was straight and that the man was still running Harvey leapt back to his car, reversed it violently, then trod on the accelerator and tore out into the traffic in pursuit.

He would probably have accomplished his object except for the fact that he almost ran into a police patrol car in his hurry. By the time he had unconvincingly explained where the fire was his quarry was lost to sight.

'This is preposterous!' he fumed, as the officer eyed him impartially and made notes. 'You've made me lose an important business connection. You'll smart for this, my friend! Or maybe you don't know who I am?'

'Only too well, Mr. Bradman. Funny business, life, when you come to think of it.'

'Oh, so you're a philosopher, eh?' Harvey glared. 'And what's so funny about it, anyway?'

'Only that last night you saved a woman and an express from possible death and accident; then this morning you drive to the public danger. Looks as though we're all creatures of circumstance, sir.'

Harvey mouthed but he did not say anything — and five minutes later he drew up again outside the block of flats to find Vera on the pavement, stunningly dressed and made up, but eyeing him with ill-controlled fury.

'You crazy?' she enquired coldly.

'Me, darling?' Harvey hopped out beside her. 'No, not yet. Never can tell, though.'

'Just what I was thinking. I was coming down the entranceway there to meet you when you turned tail and drove off like a lunatic. What bit you?'

'I — er — happened to see somebody I knew.'

'Whom you considered more important than me?'

'Not at all.' Harvey gestured vaguely. 'Just one of those things — But hop in, darling; we'll be late for lunch.'

Vera hesitated and then gracefully draped herself in the wide front seat, shutting the door with a decisive slam. Harvey gave an anxious glance about him, half expecting to see his double suddenly reappear and probably blow things sky-high — but no such thing happened. There was only the quiet sunshine, the men and women going back and forth, and the glances at the huge land cruiser that called itself a sports car.

It was now, as he drove soberly through

the traffic with the still not entirely mollified Vera at his side, that Harvey had a chance to think — and the more he thought the more puzzled he became. It had been queer enough to behold his double in this very region, but how on earth had he known that Harvey would come to that particular place?

'Darned queer,' Harvey muttered, unconsciously thinking out loud.

'What is?'

He had forgotten Vera for the moment. Now he quickly regained his normal mood.

'Sorry, just working something out. And don't be so brusque with me, Vee. After all, I am a hero.'

'Yes. I suppose so.'

'Suppose so! The paper said so, didn't it? And you said so yourself!'

'Right again — but that sudden giant strength of yours has me baffled. And I never knew you were a clever enough car mechanic to put a stalled car right in a few minutes. Yet you apparently did it last night.'

'I was just in the mood. As I said

earlier, there are a lot of things about me you don't know.'

'I will when we're married,' Vera said.

Since the High Sierra Restaurant had been reached Harvey let the subject drop — but it was plainly still worrying Vera for she asked a blunt question when they were seated at their favourite table.

'What on earth took you in the direction of Upper Namos last night, and at that hour? And without your car! There was no mention of it in the newspaper: you drove the reporter's car after you'd fixed it.'

'Uh-huh,' Harvey agreed, and he had time to think what came next whilst he gave his order to the waiter. 'Matter of fact I wanted to get away from things. You upset me a lot and I just walked and walked after I'd garaged the car — '

'Walked twenty miles!' Vera exclaimed blankly. 'You just couldn't! And Upper Namos is that far away because I've looked up all about it.'

'I have more strength than you think, my dear. Remember the car I pulled free. And it isn't what I call good form to question an act of extreme bravery so closely.'

'Sorry.' Vera relaxed into her sweetest smile. 'It's just that I'm having an awful struggle to reconcile the whole thing.'

'So am I,' Harvey muttered, and thanked heaven that the waiter returned at that moment.

For a while nothing further was said, then as he came to the end of the soup Harvey caught a glimpse of a face looking at him intently just above the costly curtains, which hung half way up the restaurant windows. It was himself again!

And the moment he noticed the face the face withdrew quickly.

'Back in a minute, Vee,' Harvey gasped, surging to his feet so violently he all but upset her soup plate into her lap. 'Something most important — '

Blundering into chairs, waltzing around an approaching waiter, Harvey shot to the swing doors — and was gone. Vera sat speechless, then finally catching herself with her mouth wide open she gave a little cough and recovered herself as the waiter reappeared. He looked about him.

'Mr. Bradman will be returning, Miss Maynard?'

'I hope,' Vera answered vaguely — but when Harvey did at last reappear fifteen minutes had elapsed. He was hot, dusty, and his immaculate suit was soiled with streaks of dirt. Pushing back his tumbled hair he settled again at the table.

'Sorry,' he apologized meekly, and Vera shrugged.

'Oh, don't mind me. I delayed the sweet in the virtuous hope that you would one day come back. Feeling better now?'

'Vee, you don't understand — '

'How did you guess?'

'I'm sorry, and I realize it must be very confusing to you, but there was a very real reason why I had to dash out. It was a very important businessman I've been trying to contact. The same chap I saw when I drove away suddenly from your flat this morning. I chased him this time down all the back streets and even through an old granary — but he got away.'

'Got away? What on earth are you talking about? What is he — a pick-pocket?'

'I mean he — he gave me the slip. More simply I lost track of him.'

Silence. Harvey cleared his throat, straightened his tie, then tried to eat. He gave it up finally and called for drink instead. Vera clung to her decision to have the sweet.

'I have the ring, Vee,' Harvey said at last. 'Now seems as good a time as any to put it on your — '

'What do you mean by an important businessman?' Vera interrupted, with cold deliberation. 'You never did a stroke of business in your life. It certainly couldn't be anything connected with the Bradman Shipping Line because you don't know the difference between a man-o'-war and a rowing boat.'

'Nothing to do with business, Vee. I mean — science.'

Harvey wondered for a moment why he had said that, and then it occurred to him it must have been because scientific things were all that interested him — as third place to Vera and hard drinks.

'Science?' Vera repeated, looking more

dazed than ever. 'When did you ever have anything to do with science?'

'Well, I — that is . . . it interests me. Stars, planets, and what-have-you. I'm pretty interested in nuclear physics, too. Quite a hobby! Ask Peters next time you meet him.'

'I think not. Peters is so thick with you he'd say anything. And that you should suddenly desert me, then return here like something the dog dragged in, all to chase a vague scientific businessman is beyond all reason. You can keep that ring.'

'What! Now look, Vee, you promised that if I — '

'I'm exercising a woman's privilege to change her mind. You may have performed one brave act, but it's certainly gone to your head.'

Harvey finished his drink disconsolately. Vera gave him a troubled glance, hesitated, then looked at him again:

'Oh, all right,' she sighed. 'Don't look so pathetic. I'll keep my promise. Where's the ring?'

Harvey brightened, slipped it on her finger, and then kissed it gently.

'Crazy I may be, hero I may be, but I certainly am in love with you, Vee,' he murmured. 'I shan't dash off again like that, believe me, even if he should reappear.'

'Who? The scientific business man who escapes down back streets?'

Harvey did not reply. He was getting confused in the head again and it was not altogether the drink, either. Who the devil was this mystic double of himself? Couldn't be an illusion of his own mind because the woman reporter had seen him too.

'Would you be willing,' Vera asked, 'to drive out to Upper Namos when we leave here and have a look at the spot where you performed your masterpiece? I'd rather like to see it.'

'No,' Harvey pleaded. 'Not that, Vee! There might be folk about there, especially the old girl who runs the gate, who'd want to praise me for my bravery. I couldn't stand that. In fact,' he hurried on, 'they are pretty well bound to be repairing the gate and I might get questioned. I don't want my identity to be revealed.'

'Why not?'

'Well, I'm modest that way.'

'Funny to me,' Vera said, 'that that woman correspondent did not recognize you. You are well known in the social whirl, and your face has graced, or disgraced, quite a few of the society magazines. So why didn't she realize who you were? Or why didn't the news editor who must be up in these things?'

Harvey was silent since this was a point that had so far escaped him. Most strange that he had not been recognized — unless at close quarters there were things about his double which made it evident he was not Harvey Bradman.

'Might go and have a word with that woman correspondent, or ring her up,' Vera suggested. 'I am more than willing to admit that you performed a brave deed, but I don't agree with having your name suppressed. There are quite a lot of lounge lizards in our set who think you're one hundred percent playboy: I want them to know my future husband is a man of courage, great strength, and resource.'

'They will know it from the photo,' Harvey said weakly. 'They'll recognize me, and my modesty will strengthen the point.'

'Mmmm,' Vera mused, and Harvey waited uneasily; then at her next words his face cleared. 'Very well, my hero, if you want it that way. After all I suppose it's your own affair. We might drop in at Harry's for the afternoon: he's throwing one of his interminable parties. Be an excellent chance to air our engagement.'

'Done!' Harvey agreed in relief, and looked around him for the waiter.

2

The impossible fingerprints

It was at the normal time of one a.m. that Harvey finally arrived home again and, as usual, Peters was awaiting him, the salary he received making his nocturnal duties well worthwhile.

'We are cheerful tonight, sir,' he commented, taking Harvey's hat and coat. 'Would I be correct in assuming that Miss Maynard accepted you?'

'You would — but she accepted me with reservations. Things have been happening.'

'Indeed, sir? You wish to tell me about them whilst you refresh?'

'Definitely!'

And over a few sandwiches and a 'scarlet lady' Harvey related the various incidents in which he had been involved with his double. Peters, following his custom, did not interrupt, and by the time Harvey had finished there was a deep frown on Peters' forehead.

'Most remarkable, sir — most. And you never got within talking distance of this double of yours?'

'Great heavens, no! The man travels as though he is jet-propelled! But what chiefly gets me down is how he knows where I am going to be when I've never given the slightest clue. Next thing I know he'll be turning up here!'

'I rather wish he would, sir, and then we might come to grips with the situation. Obviously this goes beyond a mere coincidence. Somebody of identical appearance to you is studying your actions and, possibly, trying to frighten you.'

'Well if that's the idea it's a total failure. I'm not scared: just exasperated. I'm also in the devil of a spot because if Vee ever sees this double she'll put two-and-two together and bang will go my halo of heroism.'

For a long time Peters was silent, then he gave a sigh.

'I am afraid, sir, that there is very little

we can do until this individual shows up again in such a way that we can talk to him, trap him, or otherwise get him to explain himself. Since he has not yet revealed himself to Miss Maynard, let us hope that he will continue to be as considerate.'

'Let us hope,' Harvey agreed, and upon that the subject dropped. Harvey retired to bed, but his slumber was broken by recurring mental pictures of the man who was the image of himself. As Peters had said, this business was no longer in the nature of a coincidence: it was a positive menace.

However, as several more days passed without the double putting in an appearance — and Vera had melted into sweet endearments as Harvey no longer dashed hither and yon without a reasonable explanation — it began to look as though the mystery of the double was over.

Then came the real punch to the solar plexus, and it hit Harvey as he was leaving his home to keep an evening date with Vera. A newspaper-vendor was passing the gate just as Harvey walked out to his car. He caught one glimpse of the front page, half concealed by the man's arm, but it was sufficient to freeze Harvey in his tracks. There he was again, with a different photograph this time.

'Hey!' Harvey cried, gesticulating. 'Newspaper, please!'

The man turned immediately and came hurrying up. Harvey gave a coin far in excess of the actual cost, and was too absorbed to bother with change. In fact he was too absorbed for anything. He forgot all about carrying on to his car at the kerb: he returned into the house, or rather as far as the porch, where he stood with a thumb on the bell.

'Anything wrong, sir?' Peters asked in surprise, as Harvey drifted into the hall.

Harvey made no answer. He handed over the newspaper and Peters read it slowly —

SCIENTIST DENOUNCES WOMANKIND

Dr. Boris Carter, an American metaphysical scientist, who has recently come to this country — and who on his first night in this country saved a woman from death and an express train from accident — today addressed a conference of psychologists at the Bureau of Applied Science in North London.

Dr. Carter had some very trenchant observations to make concerning womankind generally, which he stated were based on his own careful analysis. He is quite convinced that the quality of selfishness, usually referred to as a failing of the male, is far more prevalent amongst the females — and the higher in the social scale the woman happens to be the greater the selfishness.

He also stated that women as a whole are little better than cattle with the power to reason — a mental gift entirely wasted on them since no woman has ever yet reasoned with any pretension to logic.

Dr. Carter created uproar amongst many women psychologists in his audience, but he still clung to his point and calmly answered all questions that were directed at him.

This is the first public address Dr. Carter has ever made, his time up to now having been spent in seclusion whilst he studied the problem of womankind.

'Oh, dear!' Peters exclaimed, with a horrified glance. 'This has indeed put the cat amongst the pigeons! If Miss Maynard should chance to read this — '

'I've got to stop her at all costs,' Harvey decided, banging his fist on the hall table. 'Whether she takes that paper or not I can't say — I'll do what I can to head her off.'

'Yes, sir, I should.'

Peters was left to think the problem out as best he could and reconcile the name of Boris Carter with Harvey Bradman. Meantime Harvey drove hell-for-leather to Vera's flat, and the maid admitted him. The moment he set eyes on Vera he realized from her mood that so far all was well.

'You're late,' she said. 'I've had my

things on once and then took them off again when you didn't show up. I wish you'd try and be more punctual. What kept you?'

'Peters,' Harvey lied. 'He bungled things with my dress suit. Anyway, let's be going.'

Vera nodded and moved from the lounge, presumably to fix up the final details with her maid to help her. Harvey gave an uneasy glance about him and then looked at the radio. It was possible 'Dr. Carter''s arresting statements might find their way into the radio news bulletins. Without his photograph that wouldn't matter much, unless the incident with the level crossing was referred to.

'Hell, no,' Harvey whispered, and moving to the cabinet he lowered the back, snipped with his cigar cutter at the main cable inside, then replaced the back and tried to look innocent. By the time the set was fixed again Carter would no longer be news.

And the television? Harvey's eyes strayed to the big cabinet model in the corner. What were the chances of Carter appearing there? No telling — but if he did . . . And another main wire to the cathode-ray tube finished up bisected. Harvey put his cigar cutter away and gave a guilty survey around him. At the close of it his heart nearly stopped. There was the very paper on a side table, possibly brought in by the maid and not yet opened.

Instantly Harvey had reached it, thankful that it had been folded in such a way that his — or Carter's — photograph was on the underside. He looked around him for a place to be rid of the incriminating issue, then as he heard Vera's approaching voice he made desperate efforts to cram the paper into his coat pocket.

'Everything ready,' Vera announced, entering in her latest fur coat and model hat. 'Jane, I'll be back by — Harvey, what in the world are you doing?'

Harvey paused in his frantic wriggling and then gasped as in withdrawing his hand from his pocket he inadvertently brought the paper with it. It dropped flat on the carpet, his own photograph face upwards.

'Why, that's my evening paper from the side table there!' Vera exclaimed, coming forward. 'What are you trying to do with it?'

'Nothing, darling, nothing at all.' Harvey picked it up and airily folded it, but his general actions were so unnatural Vera's suspicions were instantly aroused.

'Harvey, there's no earthly reason why you should behave like that with my evening paper! I'll want to read it later on — Give it to me.'

'It's a bit knocked about,' Harvey admitted, turning it over so the front page was towards himself. 'I'll buy you the *Standard* when we get outside — '

'I don't want the *Standard*: I want that!' And being the kind of woman she was Vera took it. Harvey, rather than precipitate a rough-house — particularly before the maid who had just come into view — released his grip and then waited dully for the storm to break.

Vera took one glance at the photograph, then a second one. After which she read the column concerning Dr. Carter. Her mouth tightened slowly and at length she glanced at the maid. 'Leave us, Jane, please.'

'Yes, m'm. But I wanted to ask you about the — '

'Later, Jane.'

The maid went into the domestic region of the flat and Vera's eyes took on a steely glitter.

'That,' Harvey stated flatly, 'is not me!'

'Don't be an idiot! Of course it is you! I'd know you anywhere and this photograph is quite sufficient. Dr. Carter indeed!'

'Now look, Vee, this Dr. Carter is a different person altogether — '

'I don't believe it! That is, unless you've got some way of proving it to me.'

'That is the difficulty,' Harvey muttered. 'I haven't seen you during today, otherwise I'd have the perfect alibi. You said you were doing something with the Women's Help League, or whatever it is, and wanted to postpone our meeting until tonight — '

'Never mind what I have been doing:

what about you? From the look of things you've been having women in general and me in particular under some kind of — of mental microscope! No wonder you wouldn't attach your own name to a statement like that!'

'Vee, you've got this whole thing wrong — '

'How can I have? It says it's the same man who did that level crossing stunt the other night, and you've already got me to become engaged to you on the strength of that. What kind of a fool do you take me for, Harvey?'

Harvey was silent, cursing under his breath.

'So women are selfish, are they?' Vera resumed after a moment. 'The higher the social scale the greater the selfishness! Couldn't have directed it more at me if you'd tried, could you? Little better than cattle! Why, you — '

'I didn't say any of those things and I'm not Dr. Carter!' Harvey shouted.

'Then who was it saved that woman reporter?'

'Dr. Carter I suppose,' Harvey confessed miserably. 'I didn't do it, Vee. I just cashed in on his amazing resemblance to me.'

'That,' Vera declared after a moment, 'I do not believe! You couldn't stoop that low! No, you're this Dr. Carter all right, using an alias so that you can air your views about so-called scientific topics. I suppose you enjoy the sensation. The only redeeming feature in the whole thing is that you did perform one act of heroism as Dr. Carter, even though you were smart enough at that time not to give your name. Just how long has this been going on? Obviously not long since it says here you never made a public address before.'

Harvey spread his hands helplessly. 'I keep on telling you: this Carter fellow is not me. Let's go to the Bureau of Applied Science and make full enquiries. That ought to convince you!'

'I'm not going anywhere! On the one hand if you are not this Dr. Carter you became engaged to me by a trick; and if you are Dr. Carter I'll have nothing to do with a man who thinks things like that about women! This, Harvey, is the finish!'

Harvey opened his mouth to speak, then closed it again as he realized Vera had put the engagement ring in his palm. He looked at it, then at her — but with a toss of her head she turned away from him.

'All right,' he said quietly, pocketing the ring. 'I've told you the truth about myself and confessed my black sin. If you won't take me on the strength of that I may as well go. I'll send in a repairman to fix your radio and television.'

Vera swung. 'What on earth for? There's nothing the matter with them.'

'There wasn't, but there is now,' Harvey replied ambiguously. 'So-long, Vee. It was grand while it lasted.'

He left the flat and closed the door decisively; then with his face grim he hurried outside to his car and thereafter drove as fast as possible to the Bureau of Applied Science. He had rather expected to find the great building closed — but instead the windows were bright with lights along one block, possibly in readiness for night school students.

In a matter of moments Harvey was

inside the building. One or two fast moving young men and women, clutching files under their arms, glanced at him and then fled either along the wide hallways or up the broad staircase — until one young man, plainly a master, came to a stop as he saw Harvey looking about him.

'Why, Dr. Carter!' he exclaimed in delight, coming forward. 'This is a pleasure indeed! I never expected you would return. You said you were going into deep research on ions, remember?'

'Did I?' Harvey asked vaguely; then, 'Oh yes, of course! So I did! Well. I — er — thought I — '

'Come along to my office, sir. There are quite a few matters I would like to discuss with you. In fact I'd rather like to tempt you back for special lectures on meta-physics — just for the night school students. You know how it is.'

'Indeed, yes,' Harvey assented, terrified as to what would happen next. In fact, all the time the young teacher had been talking he had been drifting towards one of the corridors, and perforce Harvey had kept pace with him.

'Your lecture on women certainly raised a furore in the evening papers,' the teacher smiled. 'Only this afternoon when you gave it, yet editorials are already out either praising or vilifying you.'

Harvey smiled unconcernedly. 'One of things inseparable from a new theory, my friend.'

'Indeed, yes. Come in, Dr. Carter.' The teacher had reached his office. He threw the door open, switched on the light, and motioned Harvey inside. There seemed to be some puzzlement on the teacher's face concerning Harvey's evening dress, but he did not comment upon it.

'Just why did you come back to the college, doctor?' the teacher asked, settling down and motioning Harvey to do likewise. 'I am hoping it is because you have decided to come out of your scientific lair and give us the benefit of your great metaphysical knowledge.'

'Well — er — no,' Harvey answered, musing. He could hardly say he had come to enquire about Dr. Carter. That way lay the loony-bin. 'I — I just felt that I would like to take another look around the college, or rather the Bureau.'

'Oh you can't do that. The Bureau is shut in the evenings: this is the college proper. Technical college for young science students. I am the Principal.'

'Really? I would have expected somebody much older.'

'Knowledge is not measured by years, Dr. Carter. You of all people should know that.'

'Mmmm,' Harvey acknowledged.

'You are sure you did not come back for your calculator?'

'Calculator?' Harvey started. 'Now why should I?'

'For the very simple reason that you left it behind — a not uncommon happening when a man is absorbed in theories as you must be. You left it on the desk after you had given us that wonderful thesis on stresses and strains versus inter-atomic action.'

'I did? I must be slipping. Come to think of it, though,' Harvey finished, 'I believe that is why I did return here. I know I had an objective, but when I reached here I forgot what it was. Oh, thank you.'

He took the calculator as the teacher handed it to him from his desk drawer. An idea was buzzing around in Harvey's mind, and he wanted to get out of here as quickly as possible.

'This being settled,' he said, rising, 'there is not much point in my staying any longer.'

'You mean you won't say a few words to the night students? They'd be fascinated.'

'Doubtless — but I never make a speech without notes. I like to have everything worked out in detail before I begin!

'You didn't use any notes this afternoon, Dr. Carter?'

'A different thing altogether: I was fully rehearsed in my subject.'

'I see.' The teacher rose and held out his hand. 'Since I can't persuade you, doctor, I can only wish you every success with your ionic experiments.'

Harvey smiled rather woodenly and took his departure with as much courteous haste as he could. Here and there on his return to the outdoors students noticed him, gave him looks of awe, and then went on their way. It happened so many times that it was plainly obvious to Harvey that he and his double must be completely identical: evidently even the dress suit visible under the unfastened overcoat did not in the least detract from his identity.

'Damned queer,' he muttered, as he settled again at the wheel of his car. 'But it's also possible that we might get a solution to all this very quickly, and bring this certain somebody into the light of day.'

The idea he had in mind was still buzzing there, and he wasted no time in getting home. Peters admitted him gravely, knowing from the time — seven-fifteen — that the evening schedule had evidently not gone according to plan.

'I gather, sir, that your efforts to placate Miss Maynard were not entirely successful?'

'Complete flop, Peters, and she gave me the ring back, in spite of my confessing to everything. However, we can skip that for the moment. I'm going to turn into a detective and find out the truth about this idiot who is impersonating me — or at any rate who is making capital out of resemblance to me.'

'Identical resemblance, sir, if I may say so,' Peters remarked. 'The whole business is completely uncanny.'

Relieved now of his hat and coat Harvey felt in his pocket and brought the calculator to view in its transparent plastic case.

'The property of Dr. Carter, Peters!' he announced in triumph.

'Very interesting, sir. Might I ask where you obtained it?'

'From the Bureau of Applied Science. I went there to make inquiries concerning Carter . . . ' and Harvey gave the whole story. Then he finished, 'It occurred to me this might have exceptional value by reason of fingerprints. Since it is Carter's own property his fingerprints might predominate. We can find out with an improved insufflator and some chalk dust.'

'Yes, sir, very possibly — but what good will it do?'

'What good? Why, if we can find a

really good set of prints I'm going to photograph them and then submit them to Scotland Yard for checking by C-3. In other words, the fingerprint department. I don't read detective fiction for nothing.'

'So I notice, sir.' Peters' cadaverous face was grave. 'I am to assume, then, that you consider this Carter person to be a criminal? You must, otherwise you wouldn't think of trying to ask the Yard for a comparison.'

'Not necessarily a criminal, but a public nuisance, especially as far as I am concerned.'

Peters reflected for a moment. 'I would advise caution, sir. In no way, as yet, has this Dr. Carter person revealed himself in the guise of a criminal. Quite the contrary. He is apparently a very provoca-tive scientist. Anything suggestive of him being a criminal would be deemed defamatory and you would find yourself in trouble.'

'I'm doing this in my own way,' Harvey interrupted stubbornly. 'No, you're the man with the mechanical mind so see what you can do to rig up our requirements.'

'With your permission, sir, I know a photographic agent who might be able to provide all we need. His shop will be closed now but I fancy I know where to contact him.'

'On your way, then. Charge everything to me.'

'If he is willing to come himself,' Peters added, 'shall I allow him to? He is an expert on microphotography, and possibly fingerprints.'

Harvey nodded. 'Get him by all means.'

Peters departed and, picking up the calculator in its protective covering, Harvey made his way to the smallest room in the big house, which he used exclusively as his den. He put the calculator on the writing table and then settled down to wait. It occurred to him presently that he was hardly dressed for the job in his impeccable evening clothes, so for once he changed without assistance. By the time he had completed the job, and finished up in slacks and a maroon windcheater, Peters had returned, in company with a pink-faced man with a bald head.

'Mr. Danvers, sir,' Peters introduced. 'Well known micro-photographer and supplier of photographic materials.'

'Good evening, Mr. Bradman.' The photographer put down a big reflex camera and collapsible stand of lamps, then shook hands. 'I've heard of you, of course, and I think I've seen your photograph recently in the papers.'

'Sure it wasn't Dr. Carter?' Harvey asked dryly.

Peters cleared his throat. 'I took the liberty, sir, of explaining the situation of your double to Mr. Danvers. Since Miss Maynard is no longer a factor in the proceedings I could not see there was any harm.'

'None at all,' Harvey agreed, and to Danvers he added, 'I am anxious to get the fingerprints of this double of mine and, if I can, find some way of getting his activities repressed. He's making my life a misery.'

'May I see the calculator, sir?' Danvers

held out his hand. Harvey handed the pocket-sized instrument over and then, with Peters, stood watching. Danvers was obviously a clean, methodical worker. He spread a neat cloth on the desktop and then from his box of tricks unloaded an insufflator and various small tins of powders. He carefully tipped the calculator out of its case without touching it. Next, screwing a lens into his eye he peered at the instrument intently, diagonal to the desk-light. 'Quite a number of prints,' he announced finally. 'Only to be expected with a calculator of course. I'll see what I can do.'

Using a mixture of chalk and mercury he went into action. This did not work out as he had hoped so he adopted aluminium powder, taking care not to disturb it. Again the lens went into his eye and he studied the powdered portions long and earnestly.

'Suitable enough to photograph, I think,' he said, and set up his reflex camera. He took several photographs, varying the light position each time — then at last he dusted away the powder and handed the calculator back to Harvey, in its case.

'Now what?' Harvey asked.

'I can tell you the result in an hour, Mr. Bradman, and you can then examine the prints for yourself. I'll make photographs suitable for submittal to Scotland Yard if that is what you want.'

'Just what I want.'

'I wonder, sir,' Peters said slowly, 'whether it would not be a good idea to have your own prints photographed as well?'

Harvey stared. 'Why the devil should I? I'm no crook!'

'Quite so, sir — but if you should wish at some future time to prove to Miss Maynard that you are not Dr. Carter it might be useful to have your own prints alongside his, with Mr. Danvers' written guarantee below them. And not only for Miss Maynard's sake, either. There might be other difficult situations which will demand proof of your innocence should this Dr. Carter perform some criminal act.'

'Good idea,' Harvey agreed promptly.

'Can you fix it, Mr. Danvers?'

'Very easily, sir.' And within ten minutes the job had been done and Danvers went on his way with the promise to return within an hour.

'And if there is no criminal record of Dr. Carter, sir?' Peters asked, raising his eyebrows. 'What then?'

'I dunno. Have to think further. Mighty good idea of yours, though, to keep my prints and his side by side. But there again we're in difficulty. If there are more than one set of prints on the calculator, as there may be since that college principal also handled it, where are we?'

'As to that, sir, a calculator is an instrument which is handled a good deal and I imagine there will be a great predominance of one set of prints, which will be Carter's.'

'You think of everything,' Harvey grinned. 'Fix me a blue atomic whilst we're waiting, will you? Have one yourself if you wish.'

'You are most kind, sir.'

Harvey drank down his blue atomic and from then on it was just a matter of waiting, and it seemed the longest hour he had ever known. Peters absented himself to the kitchen regions, taking his own blue atomic with him, and there relaxed in his shirtsleeves, trying to work out for himself possible explanations for Carter's incredible resemblance to His Nibs.

Then, at length, Danvers returned. His face was still pink but now it had a curious anxiety upon it. He had the manner of one who wants an urgent question answered immediately.

'Everything fixed?' Harvey asked quickly, as Peters showed Danvers into the den.

'As far as I am concerned, yes, Mr. Bradman.' And the expert laid several excellent photographs on the table. 'But before I go further I must ask you something. Did you at any time, when given that calculator, take it out of its case and handle it with your bare fingers?'

Harvey shook his head. 'I took care not to. Not once.'

'Then I just don't understand it. Look here.' Danvers pointed to two photographs, both of them marked with curious whirligig lines, which, in turn, were numbered. 'You see here two photographs, both of them giving an excellent outline of the thumb print. They look as though they belong to one and the same person, but that is not so. The print on the left is from the calculator, and is presumably Dr. Carter's: the print on the right is your own thumb.'

Harvey's expression became blank. 'But — but you can't mean that my prints are identical to Carter's! That just isn't possible!'

'I well know it, yet that is what my analysis shows. Line for line, loop for loop, the two prints are identical. They are both of what we call the lateral pocket loop type.'

There was silence. Harvey was quite incapable of speaking and Peters' sharp eyes were hidden behind his lowered brows.

'I have made a thorough examination,' Danvers continued, 'which has only served to increase my confusion. On the calculator are half a dozen clear prints all of which belong to the same person: there are others also from somebody else which only appear twice.'

'Be the teacher's,' Harvey said, 'from when he picked the instrument up and returned it to its case.'

'I see. I'd rather hoped they would be yours.'

'I keep telling you, I never handled the thing.'

'Then what am I to do, sir? Your prints are all over the instrument, identical to those I took specially. You must have handled it quite a lot, and recently.'

'Never.' Harvey insisted. 'There's something about this business which is downright uncanny! I suppose it is an absolute fact that no two people in the world have identical fingerprints?'

'That,' Danvers confirmed, with an odd look, 'is an absolute fact.'

Peters cleared his throat. 'I would suggest, sir, that Mr. Danvers writes the guarantee concerning these prints and — '

'Not likely!' Harvey interrupted. 'You don't think I want my prints identifying with Carter's, do you? That's the very thing I'm trying to disprove.'

'Perhaps I had better go,' Danvers suggested. 'I have done all I can and if you need me again I'll be only too happy. I'll send in my bill later.'

He left with the speed of a man who has seen something not of this world — and, indeed, that was the way Harvey was commencing to feel about it. His face proclaimed as much as Peters came stalking gravely back into the den.

'A most unique situation, sir,' he commented.

'Unique! Is that what you call it? It's impossible, Peters; utterly impossible! According to the infallible law of fingerprints, I and Carter are one and the same person!'

'Yes, sir. Which is absurd. Unless some inexplicable law of science might account for it. A kind of positive split personality whereby you are in two places at once, having two individualities, yet each one complete in itself. That would explain why this Carter person knows what you are doing and where you are intending going. His mind is also yours — '

'Even granting such a cockeyed theory,

Peters, it's dead wrong. If Carter knows about me I ought to know about him. And I don't! Not a blasted thing! Hence all this effort.'

'I would remark, sir, that the theory is not cockeyed,' Peters pointed out, his voice hurt. 'Fielding, the famous American scientist, outlined that theory many years ago. I remember reading it. Some scientists even believe it accounts for the telepathic kinship existing between identical twins.'

'This puts me in one dickens of a spot, Peters,' Harvey said nervously. 'Suppose Carter murders somebody or robs a bank, leaving prints all over the place? I could easily be accused, and no court on earth would believe me if I said I was innocent. The only answer is that the law of fingerprints it not infallible. There can be identical prints, and we're proving it.'

'Sorry, sir, but I can't agree with that. There's some other explanation — Pardon me,' Peters broke off, as the telephone in the hall rang sharply. Harvey glanced moodily towards the hall and then continued his pacing, his brows knitted. In a moment Peters returned.

'Miss Maynard, sir,' he announced. 'She would like a word with you. If I may say so, she sounds in an excellent humour.'

'She does? Wish I felt the same.'

Harvey strode out into the hall and picked up the 'phone. He deliberately kept all cordiality out of his voice.

'Hello, Vee. Thought we were washed up.'

'Oh. Why are you so contrary?' her voice demanded. 'You spend a whole hour convincing me of your powers, leaving me to think it over, then you jump to the conclusion we're all washed up. It doesn't make sense.'

'No,' Harvey agreed, starting. 'No, it doesn't.' He was on the verge of asking when he had spent an hour explaining himself, then an inner sense warned him to keep silent.

'I was much too impetuous,' Vera sighed. 'If you still think you can forgive me I'm willing to have you put the ring back on my finger.'

'I'll be damned!'

'What did you say, Harvey? Line's not very clear.'

'Neither is my head. What brought this sudden change of mood?'

'Now how can you ask a question like that after the trouble you went to convincing me of your scientific power?'

This time Harvey just stared in front of him. Vera's voice came to him again, peevishly.

'Can't you hear me, Harvey?'

'Yes, yes, darling — of course I can. I'll come right away and replace the ring. I'm just a bit bewildered, that's all.'

'Why? You stated your case clearly enough. No sensible woman could refuse you after that.'

'Couldn't she? I — I mean no, of course not. Be right over.'

Harvey put the 'phone back on its cradle and looked dumbly at Peters as he came gliding into the hall.

'Anything wrong, sir?' he asked politely. 'Forgive me, but I am interested in Miss Maynard's reactions to — '

'Peters, either she is nuts or else I am. She's completely reversed her decision

64

about me on the strength of my convincing her of my scientific power! She says I spent an hour explaining things to her.'

'Remarkable, sir. Clearly our friend Dr. Carter has put in a good word for you.'

'That's the way it looks — but how could he have been so utterly convincing as to make Vee believe that he was me? There isn't a thing she misses! He must have given a classic performance.'

'Evidently, sir. It is at least interesting to note that his intentions towards you are not entirely hostile. In this case he has evidently straightened out your difficulties. I would suggest you see Miss Maynard immediately. She may be able to reveal something.'

Harvey nodded somewhat stupidly and then looked down at himself.

'Can't go in these togs. We'll probably go and celebrate or something. Give me a hand back into my monkey suit, Peters.'

'Delighted, sir.'

3

Alien doppelganger

When Harvey arrived at Vera's flat he found her all smiles, which only served to deepen his confusion. She was still in her evening gown, but the fur coat and model hat were not in evidence.

'Come in, darling.' She caught at Harvey's arm. 'Do sit down. Can you honestly forgive me for being so dense?'

'Well, I — I suppose we're all pretty dense sometimes.'

Harvey gave a weak smile and sat down. He was still wearing his overcoat but the maid had taken his hat. Vera went over to the cocktail cabinet and poured out drinks. As she brought them across she asked:

'It won't be against your scientific principles to drink, will it? After all you had to say, and the high-flown things of which you spoke, I'm sort of wondering.'

'Believe me, Vee, I've a long way to go before I'll refuse a drink! I — er — hope my scientific explanation didn't prove too much for you to grasp?'

'By no means. For that matter there were no really deep scientific technicalities, were there?'

'No. Of course not.' Harvey swallowed down his drink and tried to fathom how to find out what he really was supposed to have discussed.

'Anyway,' Vera went on blithely, 'it's all settled. We forgive and forget and I become engaged to the famous scientist who hides his brilliance under the guise of a playboy.'

Harvey's glass dropped from his nerveless fingers to the carpet. Vera noticed it but apparently attached no importance to it. As Harvey picked it up she added:

'Honestly, Harvey, you ought to have told me. I'd have understood. It would have saved a lot of misunderstandings.'

'Mmmm. But I thought you'd thrown me overboard because of the things I said about women.'

'I did at first, until you made the position so clear. I realize now that, from the elevated scientific point of view, seventy-five percent of women are indeed incapable of logical thinking. Myself amongst them.'

'I certainly must be some talker to have convinced you of that.'

Vera only smiled and Harvey waited for the next; then as nothing happened he suddenly remembered the ring and produced it. Gently he put it back on Vera's finger.

'And this time nothing is going to upset things,' she said firmly. 'To think that I nearly threw away the chance of becoming the wife of so brilliant a scientist! I'm so glad, Harvey, to discover that you are not just a gin-drinking lounge lizard. You really do use your brains, after all.'

'Surprising how slow they are sometimes, though,' Harvey sighed. 'Do you know, I've almost forgotten already what I talked to you about! My scientific side only seems to work at intervals.'

'It will all come back to you in time,' Vera said. 'I am certainly not clever enough to remember any of it — '

She glanced up as the telephone rang. 'All right, Jane, I'll get it,' she told the maid, as she appeared.

'Miss Maynard?' came the mellifluous voice from the other end of the wire. 'Has Mr. Bradman arrived yet? This is Peters speaking.'

'Oh, Peters! Yes, he's here.'

Harvey looked up sharply and took the telephone as Vera handed it to him.

'Can you hear my voice on this low pitch, sir?' came Peters' hoarse enquiry.

'Just about. What's wrong, anyway?'

'Everything, sir. He's here!'

Harvey started. 'Er? Who? Have you been drinking, Peters?'

'Certainly not, sir — but you'd better get back right away. He's waiting for you.'

'Who is?' Harvey nearly shouted.

'Dr. Carter, sir, in person. I thought it was you when I opened the door: now I've just found that it wasn't — I mean isn't. He told me so. The fact that I'm talking to you now proves it too.'

'Oh.' Harvey's voice was weak. 'Yes, I'll come.'

He rang off and turned to look at Vera. At her enquiring glance he gave an uncomfortable smile.

'You remember the scientific business associate, Vee? The one I dashed after?'

'Certainly I do. What about him?'

'He's called at my place with some urgent business and I'm afraid I just have to see him.'

'Why be afraid? Of course you must see him.'

Harvey looked astonished. 'This is a very different reaction to the one you had last time.'

'That was before I realized that your high eminence in science makes it necessary for you to meet all kinds of people. I'll come with you, shall I? Far as your home, I mean: I wouldn't dream of interfering with your business discussion, naturally.'

'No. I — I think it would be better if I went alone. He's a queer sort of person and might do you an injury. Had an accident once and it's made him a bit peculiar. That's why I had such a futile job trying to contact him before. We'll meet tomorrow morning, eh? Lunch as usual?'

'Anything you say.' Vera still seemed to be on top of the world and she followed up Harvey's quite perfunctory kiss with something very close to a passionate clinch.

'Okay,' Harvey said, extricating himself. 'Tomorrow it is.'

He took his hat from the maid as Vera rang for her, and after that he wasted no time getting home. A very much shaken Peters admitted him into the hall.

'It's uncanny, sir,' Peters whispered. 'I still haven't got over the shock. He's in the lounge.'

'Is he — dangerous looking?' Harvey asked uneasily.

'Quite the contrary, sir. Unless you consider that you yourself look that way. He's quiet, well mannered, and as far as I am concerned has confined himself to monosyllables.'

'I see. Well, here goes.'

Harvey braced himself and strode into the lounge, prepared for almost anything. All he received was a mild glance from a man seated in the armchair — and to Harvey at least the effect was somewhat stupefying. It was exactly like seeing himself in the mirror, except that the reflection was not obeying his particular movements.

'Good evening,' Harvey greeted, and his voice sounded a million miles away.

His double rose, attired in clothes identical to Harvey's. The only difference in Carter was that he had not divested himself of his overcoat.

'Good evening, Mr. Bradman. I think a little chat together is somewhat overdue.'

Harvey shook hands with some trepidation, but nothing happened. It was as simple a matter as shaking hands with anybody else.

'Will there be — be anything you are requiring, sir? Sirs?' Peters asked, appearing in the doorway and looking dazedly from one to the other.

'Drinks, Peters,' Harvey answered, getting control of the situation. 'I assume you will accept, Dr. Carter?'

'Gladly. Whatever you like, I like.'

'I see.' Harvey frowned to himself,

wondering what that implied, then he took his handkerchief and tied it loosely round his sleeve. 'This is to identify me, Peters,' he explained, as the manservant came over with the drinks.

'Thank you, sir. I must confess it is a little confusing.'

His task finished Peters absented himself, and it was obvious that he did so with considerable reluctance. Carter glanced towards the door and then edged forward a little in his chair.

'To clear up any doubts you may have, Mr. Bradman, let me explain immediately that I am not an enemy. All I seek on this world is sanctuary, and the time to meditate.'

Harvey's eyes sharpened. 'How do you mean — on this world?'

'Well surely it must be obvious to you that I am not a native of this world?'

'It's nothing of the kind. You look exactly like me, which means you look like a man of Earth. You talk normally; you dress as I do. There isn't a single thing to indicate that you are not of this world — ' Harvey broke off, conscious of what he was saying. 'Listen to me! Taking it for granted that you are an alien from space! I just flatly refuse to believe it.'

'That's very foolish because it happens to be true.'

'But it can't be! If you were from another world you'd arrive with a fanfare of trumpets, enormous publicity — and anyway the astronomers would have seen your space machine on its way.'

'Not if it was made of non-reflective material, and transparent, as my space-ship was.'

Harvey stared fixedly; then he took the two empty glasses and put them back on the sideboard. He knew he ought to feel scared, and yet he did not. Here, in the quiet of his own home, he was talking to somebody identical to himself who claimed he had come from outer space. It was enough to produce goose pimples. Yet it didn't. There was an easy style about Carter, a style as easy as Harvey's own.

'What planet have you come from?' Harvey asked.

'Malconeth. It is a planet a little over 11 light years from Earth.'

'That far away!' Harvey gasped. 'But — but the distance is colossal!'

'The distance does not signify. My machine travelled at many times the speed of light. Light is not the maximum speed in the universe, in spite of what some scientists think — any more than the speed of sound is the limit of speed for some of your aircraft, as was once thought to be the case. My planet has the star you call Procyon for its sun. You may know of it?'

'I do, yes,' Harvey assented, returning to his chair. 'I dabble a little in astronomy as a hobby. Not very deeply, though. My time is much occupied in — '

'Doing nothing?' Carter suggested whimsically, and Harvey glared at him.

'I can please myself what I do with my life! And let me tell you this: I strongly resent your resemblance to me! You have got me into no end of a mess with my fiancée.'

'I realized that, which is why I cleared things up for you. It is somewhat unfortunate, perhaps, that I selected as my pattern a man so well known in society as yourself. And, Mr. Bradman, it is not that I just resemble you: I am you, to the last detail, in physique. The only thing different is my mind.'

'You mean your brain, I suppose?'

'I said my mind, and that is exactly what I mean. A brain of itself is just grey tissue with no more real power to reason than that table yonder. My mind is my own, and because I am a being of Malconeth I have intelligence of a range far greater than yours.'

'Oh?' Harvey was looking cynical now. 'Conceited too, huh?'

'Not at all. On Earth here evolution is by no means at its zenith, nor will it be for many millions of years yet. On the other hand, on my world evolution had reached its limit — hence the greater knowledge. Only time begets knowledge, my friend. I am the last of my race and, as I said at first, I am seeking sanctuary and the time to meditate.'

'Meditate over what?'

'Oh, many things,' Carter answered musingly, gazing into the fire. Then he looked at Harvey directly. 'But let me start at the beginning. Mr. Bradman. About a year ago, finding myself alone on my world — and not liking it a bit — I decided to seek company. I examined all possible planets, which possessed thinking beings who might be worth a visit. We had of course been receiving and monitoring radio and television broadcasts for many years from this world of yours, and Earth was my planet of choice. Knowing of the xenophobic tendencies of Earth people, I realized though that if I arrived here in my normal physical vestment I might start a panic, or else get myself promptly killed. It was plain, then, that the best way to orientate myself was to make myself exactly like an Earthman. Accordingly, I landed at first on your satellite, from which vantage point I was able to examine the life on your planet at my leisure.'

'And out of the millions of people on Earth you had to pick me!' Harvey exclaimed bitterly.

'Whoever I had selected would have found the business just as embarrassing,' Carter shrugged. 'I selected you because your physical aura was of exactly the right type for my patterner, just as a sculptor might find a certain type of clay more suitable than another for his work.'

Harvey said nothing. He was feeling too dazed.

'All living beings emit electronic vibrations by the very fact that they are living matter,' Carter resumed. 'Sufficiently sensitive instruments can pick up the faintest of electronic vibrations over great distances — which was exactly what I did in your case. At my distance on the moon I knew you only as an electronic pattern of exactly the right type. I had no idea what you looked like physically because my telescopes were not powerful enough to reveal that much. I only knew what you were like when I put my body in the conversion-chamber of the patterner I had brought with me aboard my ship, and allowed your electronic vibrations to completely re-fashion me.'

'Surely that must have been damned painful?' Harvey demanded.

'Not at all. A freezing process destroyed

all sensation whilst my body was transfigured to be exactly like yours. When that had been done my biggest task had been accomplished. I had taken the physical identity of somebody on Earth but I had yet to discover whom. So I came to Earth from the moon, and arrived here quietly one night. I selected a very deserted spot in your desert regions so there was no chance of my being discovered whilst I worked out the remainder of my plan.'

Harvey poured more drinks and brought them across. Carter took his glass with a nod of thanks.

'I had much to do,' he explained. 'By radio-television and other methods I had to reassess the kind of planet I had reached, and the type of people inhabiting it. I found that it had not changed significantly in the eleven-year time lag since I had last studied your broadcasts reaching my home world. In particular I had to know all about the person whose body I had duplicated. Altogether, to get all the facts I needed, took me several months. Then, armed with such few special instruments as I needed, I set forth, by this time quite proficient in the language, thanks to a study of radio and television broadcasts. On the very first occasion I reached England, deliberately sinking my space-ship into a morass so it could never be found, I came upon an Earth woman in extreme danger in a car, jammed at a level-crossing. I think you know already what happened.'

'I know,' Harvey conceded dryly. 'You exhibited great strength and pulled the car free.'

'The great strength is a legacy of my normal body, twice as strong as an Earth form, the matter being more closely packed though not taking up any more actual area. On that occasion I kept my identity secret because I had not yet selected a name and I certainly was not going to use yours. However, possessing no money I had got to make some somehow. I did it by using my superior scientific knowledge, posing as a great scientist who had long been in the midst of experiments and had only just emerged to give his views. I called myself Dr. Carter and took the risk of confusion with you. Before my lecture on Earthly women I had given quite a few less important lectures, my brilliance being taken for granted, and had made a fair sum of money that way. But, all the time, I wanted to get in touch with you. So I watched you constantly, trying to determine a convenient moment to talk to you.'

'You had a couple of good chances that I can remember, but you ran for it — and how you ran!'

'I ran, my friend, because two people so identical meeting in the open in crowded streets could have made things very difficult for both of us. Sooner or later, I decided, I would meet you privately, as I am doing now.'

'You certainly always seemed to know where to find me! How did you manage it?'

'By putting my mind in 'sympathy' with your thoughts, just as you would tune in a radio station at a particular point on the dial. More plainly, I read your thoughts and therefore knew everything you intended doing, and also where you would be.'

Harvey looked uncomfortable. 'And can you read the thoughts of anybody you wish?'

'I can, but I assure you I do not. The thoughts of Earth people are so trivial they are not worth the effort of study. However, as I was saying, I established myself quite easily as a professor of metaphysics who had long been in seclusion. Also in my lecture I included a demonstration which involved the use of a calculator. I did not actually need the instrument, but had I been seen to make the calculations mentally, that might have aroused amazement and suspicion in my audience. That I left it behind was quite accidental, and partly of course because I had no actual need of it. But I realized from your thoughts — when I 'tuned in' to see how you were faring — that you were definitely getting yourself into deep water. I also saw that your lady friend, Miss Maynard, would have nothing more to do with you.'

'On the strength of which you called upon her as me, in identical clothes?'

'I did. The clothes were carried in your

thoughts so that presented no problem to me. Arriving at Miss Maynard's flat I quickly read her mind, discovered what parts of it were amenable and receptive and then went to work. In a matter of an hour I had opened the pathway for you again. Miss Maynard is convinced you are a famous scientist by the name of Dr. Carter, that you have adopted the alias to pursue your hobby, and that your playboy attitude under your own name is only a means of relaxation.'

'You even convinced her of the truth of that astonishing lecture of yours — about women being little better than cattle and with no idea how to reason logically.'

Carter smiled reflectively. 'The reporters got my lecture somewhat mixed, I'm afraid. I certainly said that women are mentally inferior, but I also included men in that category. That fact was not made clear. In fact, compared to myself, I find all men and women distinctly low in the scale of intelligence. I do not think it was so much that Miss Maynard accepted my theory about women as that she was compelled to.'

'You mean mental compulsion was used? Hypnotism?'

'Of sorts. I felt I owed it to you to straighten things out, so I did so. Henceforth, as far as Miss Maynard is concerned, anything that I do will be ascribed to you, and you may be sure that I will always act in such a way and at such a time that you are not with anybody else when it happens. It need never be known that you and I are separate entities, though at one in physical vestment.'

'All very well for you, Dr. Carter, but what about me? If I am suddenly confronted with the need to perform a scientific miracle, how am I going to do it?'

'Simply excuse yourself for the moment and contact me. I will always stand by you, chiefly for my own sake.'

'And where will you be?'

Dr. Carter gave an odd glance. 'Now, that is a matter which we must discuss, Mr. Bradman. Our lives are so completely interlocked we cannot afford secrets from each other.'

'That,' Harvey remarked dryly, 'I find

damned funny! You can read my thoughts so obviously I can have no secrets from you — but where do I come in? I'm simply a doormat as far as you are concerned.'

'Believe me, I do not entertain any such view about you. To come back to the point: my main difficulty on this world is to have somewhere quiet where I can meditate and perhaps perform an experiment or two: my second difficulty is in sufficient money, since obviously I cannot go on lecturing and performing what appear to be scientific miracles indefinitely — '

'Just what sort of miracles are you talking about? Since I am supposed to be capable of performing those self-same miracles hadn't I better know what you've done?'

'I do not propose to go into details, but at the Bureau of Applied Science, whilst giving my lecture, I turned water into ice by metaphysical means alone, despite the fact that the room temperature was approximately seventy degrees Fahrenheit. I also caused one metal to pass through another without any material intermediary. Such feats are purely mental science, which I know places me ahead of all the scientists on Earth today. Those feats henceforth will be ascribed to you. When you are asked to repeat them, in order to maintain the reputation I have built up for you, get in touch with me.'

'And again I ask — where?'

'You own Denham Towers in Buckinghamshire, Mr. Bradman. I rather thought I might domicile myself there. At the moment I am registered at the Darlington Hotel in London here, a most unsuitable place for my activities.'

'And you think you ought to become my guest in my country home?'

'If I am to support you, yes. If you try to exist without my support, in face of the many scientific 'miracles' I may yet perform, you are liable to find yourself in difficulty.'

Harvey reflected. He was by no means a brilliant man, but even he could detect a subtle plan whereby he was subservient to this compelling being who had stolen his physical vestment and could easily dominate his will.

'You see,' Carter added quietly, relaxing again in his chair, 'I need a quiet place, as I told you, and I also need money. You have both. In return for those I am giving you a reputation second-to-none amongst present day scientists and restoring you to the woman you love. Could anything be fairer than that? I shall always keep away from you so your wife-to-be can never know the secret, and you — utilizing me — can have your name made so famous you will go down in history. That is the bargain I propose.'

Harvey got to his feet and rang the bell. Turning, he explained, 'I would like my manservant to hear this proposition. I rely a great deal on his judgment.'

'You should cultivate the habit of relying on your own judgment, Mr. Bradman. It is far more satisfying.'

Harvey did not comment. Presently he glanced up as Peters entered.

'You rang, sir?' He glanced for identification towards the handkerchief about Harvey's sleeve.

'I did, Peters. My double here has a

suggestion to make. Since it closely involves me it will also involve you. I'd like you to hear it and pass unvarnished judgment. Think of yourself as an advisor, not a manservant.'

'I appreciate the compliment, sir, and will do my best.'

Dr. Carter was smiling a little to himself, and he was still smiling when he had finished explaining his proposal. Peters' saturnine face did not display any emotion, but it was obvious he was doing some pretty fast thinking.

'I believe, sir, that the proposal is too disadvantageous to yourself,' he said finally, looking at Harvey. 'To quote from Western parlance, Dr. Carter will hold all the aces.'

'So I think.' Harvey was nodding profoundly.

'Naturally,' Carter said, 'you are entitled to your opinion, but can you suggest an alternative? The reputation of Dr. Carter, who henceforth will be known only as Mr. Bradman, has been created, and he must live up to it. If he doesn't the scientific world will laugh him to scorn and his fiancée will turn him down once and for all. You will lose everything, Mr. Bradman, except perhaps your fortune. I rather think you will prefer to shine as a scientific genius than as a somewhat mindless consumer of alcohol.'

Harvey gave a start. 'Now look here — ' He stopped dead and gave a sigh. 'He's right, Peters,' he said. 'Vee thinks I'm a genius. I can't let her go: she means too much to me. Anyway Dr. Carter's demands are not impossible to grant, are they?'

'I imagine not, sir.' Peters seemed puzzled by Harvey's sudden about-face, until he thought he understood the relentless stare in Carter's eyes.

'The east wing of Denham Towers has been closed up for years,' Harvey continued. 'No reason why Carter shouldn't have it placed at his disposal.'

'Most kind of you,' Carter smiled, rising. 'That would be all I need — I believe there is a basement to the east wing, too?'

'How did you — ' Peters began, but Harvey waved him into silence.

'There is a basement, yes, but what would you want with that?'

'Oh, just a place to potter around in and experiment. I take it then that you are agreeable? I may become a permanent guest at Denham Towers, everything provided, in return for which I shall always be at your beck and call?'

'That seems to be it.' Harvey agreed. 'What will you do? Fend for yourself?'

'I hardly consider that necessary, or desirable. I have no intention of wasting my valuable time on such mundane things. Your manservant can surely look after both of us?'

Peters' eyebrows rose a little and Harvey looked surprised.

'Buckinghamshire is quite a way from here, Carter.'

Carter smiled. 'Mr. Bradman, you are fully intending to marry Miss Maynard any day now — No, don't trouble to deny it because I know exactly of your intentions. You will go for your honeymoon and then return. To here? Perhaps. But a word in Miss Maynard's ear from you — or me — would make her far more wishful to live at Denham Towers, with perhaps occasional residence here. That, I think, is the best solution.'

'But — but if we live at the Towers as well we'll be bound to collide!' Harvey objected. 'That, you promised me, would never happen.'

'Nor will it. You and your wife will inhabit the modern wing of the Towers, and I will stay secluded in the old wing. And, as the saying is, never the twain shall meet. The only go-between will be Peters here and he, I am sure, will be the soul of discretion.'

Peters, not being in possession of all the facts concerning the dominant being from the solar system of Procyon, did not attempt to speak, but his expression revealed he was none too pleased with the suggestions put forth.

'Settled, then?' Carter asked at length.

'Er — yes.' Harvey gave a shrug, feeling he was in a corner.

'Splendid! Henceforth you have nothing to fear — though it is of course understood that whatever I do to enhance your reputation as a scientist I shall do, and you can always call on me in return. You will be a great man, Mr. Bradman, albeit by proxy. That being settled, go ahead and marry your lady-love. I will take up my residence in Denham Towers tonight.'

'Tonight!' Harvey exclaimed blankly.

'Why not? Delay cannot afford anything useful, and I am anxious to leave London so you may have a clear field and not be in danger of conflicting with me. I am sure Peters will drive me over to the Towers.'

'I am not a chauffeur, sir.' Peters observed coldly.

'Possibly not, but you can drive a car — and well. Your mind tells me as much. Mr. Bradman will be able to manage until he departs from his honeymoon. I really need a servant far more than he does. I am not as yet fully initiated in the ways of Earth people.'

This time Peters really stared, and the stare gradually transferred itself to Harvey.

'Better do as he says, Peters,' Harvey advised. 'He is not of this world.'

'Not — not of this world, sir? Then might I ask — '

'It's a long story, Peters. Get him to tell it to you on the way to the Towers. You'll realize then that he is in a position to make us do exactly as he wants.'

Peters loosened his collar slightly with one finger.

'Then it is your wish, sir, that I drive Mr. Carter to the Towers and wait on him until you and — er — Mrs. Bradman arrive there?'

'That's it,' Harvey agreed, a faraway look in his eyes, and only when the door had closed behind his double and Peters did he realize how completely he had been mesmerized into making most of the statements he had.

4

Mysterious machinery

The following day, still feeling utterly helpless without Peters at his side, Harvey kept his luncheon date. During the meal he took good care not to breathe the vaguest hint concerning the real facts.

'Now that we're resolved to be married, Vee, I see no point in delaying things,' he said. 'It's for you to name the day, and sooner the better.'

'Why the desperate hurry?' she asked curiously.

'There are many reasons. I have certain scientific obligations to fulfill and I must pick the quietest period for our honeymoon. I thought if we were married next Monday by special license it wouldn't be too soon.'

Vera hesitated. 'I'm not so sure about that. I wanted a really big society wedding with all the trimmings — '

'I know, but that would take a long time, and I honestly cannot delay things to that extent. I've a reputation to keep up, remember. We can honeymoon in the south of France and then take up residence in Denham Towers — '

'That great big rambling country place of yours! I'm not so sure I want that, Harvey.'

'I'm afraid it's the only way we'll get any peace, Vee. As long as I am in London there will be constant calls on my time and we'll never get a chance to be together for long. But out in Buckinghamshire we'll be left more or less in peace. I've already sent Peters over there to make arrangements.'

Vera thought it over, and sighed, but finally agreed — and for that much Harvey felt thankful, not because he was anxious to be near to Carter but because he did not wish to disobey his orders.

So, on the following Monday, the marriage took place as arranged. It was given considerable news space, chiefly because Vera, determined not to be entirely outdone, had given the news-hounds all the information concerning Harvey's dual personality. Thus it became generally accepted that he and Dr. Carter were one and the same person — which caused more than one socialite to blink in amazement. Then away to the south of France and the honeymoon.

In the rambling depths of Denham Towers, Dr. Carter kept track of all the events by means of the radio and television. He was comfortably domiciled in the old wing, with his own bedroom and lounge. Peters, who had been given all the details of the planet Malconeth by Carter himself, kept as far away from the alien as possible though he performed all necessary duties.

It was on the evening of the wedding day that Carter detained Peters as he was about to leave the old lounge with its dark wood antique furniture and gently glow-ing fire.

'A moment, Peters. I'd like a word with you.'

Peters returned slowly. 'Sir?'

'I believe you are a very trusted servant

of your master? Almost a confidant, as one might say.'

'Yes, sir. I endeavor to give him every assistance.'

'That was not quite what I meant, Peters. I was just considering the fact that you are a close enough confidant to even have duplicate keys to his safe — back in the London residence, that is.'

'I assume you read that fact from my mind, sir?'

'Naturally.' Carter settled down in the enormous armchair and pondered for a while. The dull glow casting on his face made him exactly like Harvey, a phenomenon that Peters had still not fully assimilated.

'Peters,' Carter said at last, 'I want you to go to the town house whilst your master is away and obtain his Number Nine cheque book — the one which he rarely uses but which is nevertheless connected with his private account.'

'May I enquire your reason for this surprising request, Dr. Carter?'

'Certainly. I need money — plenty of it. The only way to get it, since my present

97

seclusion debars me from making any, is to call upon my identity with your master and sign a cheque.'

Peters stiffened. 'I would prefer not to carry out your instructions, sir. It amounts to a criminal act.'

'Don't be tiresome, Peters, and do as you're told. It must be plain enough to you that I must have money. How can I leave here when everybody knows your master and his wife are in the south of France? I am keeping my word to him not to confuse his identity with mine, so it is up to you to play your part.'

'I will only do as you request, sir, if I have the master's permission. I can ring him up at his hotel in France.'

'No doubt, but I do not consider there is any need. You can go to London this evening and carry out my instructions. I know you have the safe keys — and banish from your mind that thought about asking Scotland Yard to step in. One move like that and you, and your master and his wife, will be in a most dangerous position.'

Peters was silent for a long while in the

firelight, then he said quietly, 'Very well. sir. As you wish.'

'Good! That's all, Peters.'

Peters left like a man in a dream. He was not hypnotized, and yet he was not absolutely in control of himself. He knew he would do exactly as he had been told because he found it impossible to imagine himself doing anything else. The aura of mental compulsion that 'Dr. Carter' emanated was overpowering.

Yes, Peters went to London and returned towards ten o'clock, cheque book in his pocket. When he entered the old lounge he found Carter still in the enormous armchair, looking as though he had never moved from it — but since fresh coal had been thrown on the fire he evidently had.

'You managed it all right, Peters,' Carter said, and it was not a question but a statement. 'Light the lamps will you?'

Peters obeyed. In this wing of the old place electricity had not yet been laid on. The room filled with shadows. Carter got to his feet and came over to the table, picking up and examining the cheque book carefully. Then, evidently satisfied, he sat down and wrote out a cheque at the bureau.

'First thing tomorrow, Peters, when the bank opens, you will cash this for me. It is for immediate necessities. I shall also have other cheques to write, but they will not be your concern.'

Peters took the cheque that had been handed to him and looked at it intently. It was quite impossible to tell that it had not been written by Harvey himself.

'You are thinking, Peters, that that cheque is a forgery.' Carter looked up at him cynically. 'Believe me, it is not. Harvey Bradman and I are one person and I have all his characteristics, including his style of handwriting. I shall not need you any further, Peters.'

'Yes, sir,' Peters muttered, and departed — and in the comparative safety of the old wing kitchen regions he looked at the cheque again. It was for £50,000.

'His Nibs should never have given way to this So-an-So,' Peters muttered, putting the cheque in his pocket. 'This is only the beginning of trouble.'

Even if it was there was precisely nothing he could do about it. Carter was installed, and looked likely for remaining. Indeed Carter became quite busy during the night whilst Peters was sleeping, albeit fitfully. In the small hours of the morning Carter explored the enormous basements under the building, which travelled beneath both old and new sections. And as he explored, oil lamp in hand, he paused ever and anon to draw a plan. Until at length, towards three in the morning, he was satisfied with his investigation.

Returning to the old lounge he examined the sketches and made notes, then he went to work with complicated designs which, for all their queer outline, were plainly machines. This done he wrote letters, quite half a dozen of them, and in each letter he enclosed a cheque. Evidently not prepared to let Peters post them he stole out in the cold of the very dark night and walked to the nearest pillar box in the village — then he returned to the Towers, and to bed.

It was a few days after this before the

results began to show. There drove up to Denham Towers several enormous lorries, bearing machinery covered with tarpaulins. Peters surveyed the proceedings but took no part in them. From the vantage point of the kitchen regions he watched heavy electrical equipment being transported into the basement, after which assembly staffs went to work under Carter's directions and bedded the machinery down.

When the various jobs had been done it was evening and Peters could control his curiosity no longer. He aimed point blank questions as he served Carter with his evening meal.

'Begging your pardon, sir, but — '

'About the stuff in the basement, Peters?' Carter interrupted him.

'Yes, sir. I don't understand the purpose of it, particularly as there is no power laid on in any part of the basements.'

'There soon will be. I am carrying a feed-line from the main cable to start up the generator which you saw being taken below. I haven't finished yet, Peters. There are other machines to come, specially designed. I do not expect them for a week. It is most essential all this work should be done before your master returns with his wife, otherwise she might ask questions.'

'Little doubt of it, sir. But the purpose of it all?'

'I don't propose to explain that, Peters . . . ' and Carter began eating.

Peters hesitated. 'If I may remark it, sir, those men who brought the equipment are liable to talk. They will be saying they have seen Mr. Bradman in the Towers here, when it is well known that he is in France on his honeymoon. What then?'

Carter shrugged. 'If those men do talk, which is highly unlikely, the obvious explanation is that your master flew over from France specially to supervise the machinery job.'

'But his wife will know quite well that he didn't, sir!'

'That is a chance which has to be taken. The machinery is far more important than Mrs. Bradman, believe me.'

Peters said no more. He stood waiting until he was curtly dismissed; then he went silently along the vast corridors of the old wing and into the new. Here he looked about him somewhat nervously and picked up the telephone.

Harvey was in the hotel lounge with Vera when he heard himself being paged, after which it was not long before he was in the telephone booth.

'Oh, that you, sir?' Peters' voice sounded remote and queer. 'There are some curious happenings here at the Towers, sir, and I'm taking the risk of telling you about them.'

'Our old friend Carter, you mean?'

'Yes, sir. It's like this.' And Peters related things in brief, including the incident of the cheque book. He sounded quite breathless by the time he had finished. 'What it all means, sir, I don't know, but I'd certainly be thankful to see you in England again. The responsibility of all this is getting too much for me.'

'And you say he wouldn't explain the electrical stuff?'

'Not a word, sir — but that isn't what is

worrying me. It is the fact that everything may fall to bits — as far as you are concerned — if those engineers talk. Can you think of any way to prove that you might have flown over here for a whole day?'

'I most certainly can't — and anyway I've been with the wife most of the time. Just the same, maybe we'd better come home. I don't like the sound of what you've told me.'

'I'll look forward to your early return, sir. Now I'd better ring off whilst I'm safe.'

Harvey re-hooked the telephone and wandered out pensively into the lounge once more. Vera looked at him curiously as he resumed his armchair opposite her.

'Who was it? One of our own set sending congratulations?'

'Anything but. Something's cropped up, Vee, and I think we ought to get back to England immediately. I know it means cutting things short, but my reputation is at stake.'

'In that case of course we'll go — but can't you tell me what it's all about?'

Harvey smiled gravely. 'Top scientific

secret, Vee. You'll have to get used to my being mysterious.'

'It's worth it to be married to a man of your scientific ability.'

To this Harvey said nothing, but there and then he made the preliminary arrangements for departure. He and Vera stayed one more night, then the next day they flew over the Channel back to England. Towards noon the chauffeur was opening the limousine doors for them at the Towers.

'You're right,' Vera remarked, as she alighted. 'This country pile of yours is quiet. I don't think I'll ever get used to it.'

'Maybe it won't be so quiet as you imagine,' Harvey replied uneasily, and cast a covert glance towards Peters; and under his breath Harvey added, 'Where is he at the moment?'

'Safely pushed away in the old wing, sir. Have no fear: he will keep to his side of the bargain, though he did seem a little upset when he knew you were coming back sooner than intended.'

'What are you two doing — exchanging reminiscences?'

Vera came forward, looking vaguely astonished at the way the two men had their heads together.

Immediately Peters straightened up. 'I beg your pardon, madam — and may I say how delighted I am to welcome you as the mistress?'

'You may, Peters.' Vera gave him a somewhat knowing smile. 'I think I know you well enough to believe that everything will run smoothly.'

'Thank you, madam. I surely hope so.'

Peters excused himself somewhat hastily so that he could help the chauffeur with the luggage. Vera went on into the tremendous hall, Harvey following behind her. Without removing their outdoor things they went into the lounge. It was by no means the first time Vera had been here — Harvey had thrown many a party here in the past — but that still did not make the girl any more impressed.

'It's gloomy and dead,' she objected. 'Honestly, Harvey, I'd sooner we fixed up in London.'

'But, Vee, I'd much rather we didn't — '

'Why not?'

'I've already told you. Once in London and I'm liable to be whipped off any time on something scientific. You have no idea how many times I came close to missing my dates with you in the past for that self-same reason.'

Vera looked about her again. 'Do you suppose the old wing might be any more cheerful? It does face the south at one point and that's something.'

'The old wing?' Harvey repeated. 'Good Lord, no! It's been shut for years and it's full of cobwebs, mice, insects, and what-have-you.'

'Then it won't be for long! I'm your wife now, remember, and I don't intend to have any part of this place locked up and flea-ridden. We'll engage a full staff and then see what can be done. Yes, maybe after a few conversions here and there this can be made to look less like a mausoleum.'

Peters appeared. 'Shall I serve lunch, sir?'

'Yes, do,' Harvey assented. 'We'll just freshen up whilst you make the necessary preparations.'

And it was during lunch that Vera drifted back to her original intentions. She called Peters over to her.

'What arrangements have you made concerning a staff for this place, Peters?'

'None, madam.' He gave a vague look towards Harvey. 'I was not aware that a staff would be required. The master did not mention it.'

'Possibly slipped his mind — but I am in control of the house now and I must have efficiency. You surely do not suppose that you alone can adequately deal with a place this size, do you?'

Peters was silent, so Harvey cut in, 'No reason why he shouldn't, dear. After all, most of the rooms in the place are locked up, especially in the old wing. We ourselves won't make things very untidy.'

'I'm not just thinking of ourselves, Harvey. We'll need many a party to keep this place on its feet and save us from turning into mummies — and besides you'll need to entertain your scientific friends quite a lot. I want the whole place renovated and brought up to date. Peters, you have carte blanche to engage a staff adequate to the task.'

'Very good, madam.'

Harvey hesitated over saying something but he did not put it into words. He exchanged another look with Peters and then no more was said. Lunch was about over when Peters vanished to answer a call at the front door. He returned with a somewhat surprising announcement.

'Mr. Calmore, your bank manager, would like a few words with you, sir. I have shown him into the library.'

Calmore, viciously clean-shaven and faultlessly dressed, turned as Harvey entered the great library, his hand extended.

'This is a surprise, Mr. Calmore. What's wrong? Do sit down.'

'Thank you, Mr. Bradman. I hope you'll forgive the liberty of my calling like this: my only reason is that, as usual, I am looking after your interests. I learned from the newspapers that you were returning home today and settling here so I — '

'Yes, quite, but what is this all about?'

'I have been wondering about certain cheques which have been passing through your number nine account. Naturally, I imagine everything is in perfect order, only it seemed just a little strange that you had suddenly issued them whilst away on your honeymoon, and on an account which you rarely use.'

'In what amount are the cheques drawn?'

Calmore unfastened his brief case and handed over five cancelled checks upon which payment had been made. Harvey took them, frowning. Each check was made out to a famous engineering firm, and the amounts were considerable. There was one for £150,000, and not one of the remaining four checks was below £20,000.

'In order?' Calmore asked hopefully. 'I would prefer to be sure, Mr. Bradman. Forgeries are becoming more and more common these days.'

'Yes, they're in order,' Harvey said, musing. 'They are for scientific equipment. You may have gathered from the papers that I am interested in that profession.'

'Yes, indeed.' Calmore did not pursue

the matter since it was not his business to do so. Satisfied that he was protecting the interests of his wealthy client he shook hands and then departed. For some time afterwards Harvey stood thinking, then with a grim face he left the library and began the long perambulation into the closed wing of the Towers — until at last he arrived at the old lounge, which Carter had made his headquarters. Carter was present, apparently figuring something out on a scratchpad.

'Welcome back, Mr. Bradman,' he greeted, getting to his feet. 'I only hope your premature return will not make things too difficult for you.'

'Why should it?'

'Simply that I shall soon be having some special machinery delivered. I had hoped to manage it before you returned with your wife: as things are now you will have to explain matters to her.'

'I will — and whilst I am about it how about you explaining to me? I have five cheques here, totalling in all to over three hundred thousand pounds! What on earth do you think you're doing, using my money like that?'

'I am exercising the privilege of being your double, Mr. Bradman. I have no money of my own, so I am sure you will not mind my having some of yours? Even if you do mind it won't make any difference. I have ordered some scientific machinery, very necessary to my experiments.'

Harvey glared. 'When you referred to scientific experiments I didn't think it was going to cost me three hundred thousand! What happens if I report your action to the police? Signing another man's cheques is a criminal offence on this world.'

'You are quite a humourist, Mr. Bradman. The whole world believes now, thanks to press reports circulated by your wife, that you and I are the same person. How could you talk yourself out of that, especially when we have identical fingerprints?'

'All right, you win,' Harvey admitted moodily. 'But go easy in future, please!'

'Why? You are worth many millions. However, it is not likely that I shall need such finance again. The machinery I have ordered should serve my purpose.'

'What purpose? Since it's my money and you said we would have no secrets from each other, I'm surely entitled to know?'

'Not in this case, Mr. Bradman. It is a scientific experiment of extreme delicacy, and in any case it is of far too advanced a nature for you to understand it. Now hadn't you better be getting back to your wife before she wonders what has become of you?'

Harvey ignored the suggestion. 'I think,' he said, 'that you had better be on your guard in future, Carter. My wife has made up her mind to have this part of the Towers cleaned out and thrown open to the fresh air. When she really gets down to it there are likely to be complications.'

'Which I leave to you to prevent, Mr. Bradman. I do not intend to be disturbed, and if anybody so much as lays a finger on the equipment I have had installed in the basement I will kill them!'

'I believe you would, too,' Harvey said slowly — then without saying anything further he left the lounge and retraced his way through the labyrinth. When he got back to Vera he found her in the modern drawing room, reclining on the sofa.

'What on earth did Calmore want all that time?' she asked in surprise. 'He took long enough to sell you the Bank of England!'

'Calmore left some time ago, Vee. He came concerning some cheques for machinery I've ordered. The stuff will be delivered any time now. I've been away so long because I've been studying the basement.'

'How intriguing!'

'Not so much intriguing as essential. I've been deciding whereabouts in the basement to have my equipment put. And that brings me to something else. I want the old wing left just as it is. I don't want any staff palavering about cleaning it up.'

Vera looked annoyed. 'Where's the sense of having half the place buried in cobwebs when it can be turned to account?'

'It isn't buried in cobwebs!'

'You said it was — and rats and mice.'

Harvey sighed. 'Look, Vee, to put it

plainly I want that half of the place entirely for my own scientific purposes — and I don't want anybody to ever go in there. Not even you, unless I expressly permit it.'

'I never heard of anything so preposterous!' Vera objected. 'What in heaven's name are you going to do that demands such secrecy?'

'I am going to dabble with the basic forces of matter,' Harvey replied enigmatically. 'If you wander into the region of my activities you might become mixed up with static electricity and get yourself killed. Besides, as a scientist, I have the right to privacy.'

'All right,' Vera agreed, none too happily, 'but that does not mean a staff cannot be engaged to keep this modern part of the place up to scratch, does it?'

'By all means! Do what you like around here, but leave the other part untouched.'

Vera nodded and Harvey breathed a little more freely. He settled down in the nearest armchair. Vera watched him for a moment and then looked puzzled.

'What about your appointment?' she asked.

'What appointment?'

'I had the impression we dashed from France so that you could see somebody about a top scientific secret.'

'Oh, that! I've already fixed it over the 'phone. Now I await developments.'

'I like that! Why couldn't you have fixed things over the 'phone from France and saved us cutting short our honeymoon?'

Harvey was spared from answering this stinger by the arrival of Peters.

'Dr. Hargraves of the Association of Advanced Scientists, sir. He wishes to see you and I conducted him to the library.'

'Oh, Lord,' Harvey muttered, getting to his feet. 'All right, Peters, thank you.'

'What are you groaning about?' Vera asked. 'I'd have thought a man as famous as Dr. Hargraves, England's greatest expert on matter and energy — according to the newspapers — ought to be just the man you'd want to see. One on your own level.'

Harvey smiled weakly, did not say anything — and escaped. In the library he came face to face with Kenneth Hargraves, acknowledged to be one of the greatest physicists of his day. He was a tall, austere man with whitening hair, but his greeting to Harvey was genial enough.

'A pleasure indeed, Mr. Bradman!' he exclaimed, shaking hands. 'Or do you prefer that I address you by your scientific alias of Dr. Carter?'

'It's immaterial,' Harvey answered. 'Take a seat. Dr. Hargraves. What can I do for you?'

'Demonstrate!'

'I was afraid of — I mean, in what way?'

'I was present when you gave your famous display before the audience at the Bureau of Applied Science — a masterpiece of metaphysical control if ever there was one. Since then I have had considerable difficulty in convincing many of my colleagues who were not present that you do indeed possess the power of controlling matter. Therefore I have convened a special conference, to be made up of all those scientists — from all parts of the world — who missed your earlier feats. Might I ask you to repeat them? Needless to relate you may name your own fee.'

'Well now,' Harvey mused, 'I am immensely busy at the moment — deep in studies which I do not wish to disturb — '

'Surely you are not going to refuse, Mr. Bradman? I have banked on the fact that you will seek every opportunity to enhance your reputation.'

'Er — when is the conference?' Harvey asked.

'Tomorrow night at the Association Building — the lecture hall. There ought to be about three thousand present.'

'Will you pardon me a moment, then, whilst I consult my diary? I'll see what I can do for you.'

Harvey left the library quickly and fled through the labyrinth once again until he had reached the old lounge. Carter was present and, Harvey noticed, was dressed in clothes identical to his own.

'You don't have to say anything,' Carter said. 'I know what has happened. I'll take over from here, true to my promise to be always on hand. You will remain here until I return, whenever that may be. Understood?'

'Yes, I suppose so. How did you manage to get clothes like my own?'

'In your town home, Mr. Bradman, there are many duplicates of everything you wear. I had Peters lay in a supply for me against just such a moment as this.'

'But how do you know what has been happening? You couldn't have read it all from my thoughts that quickly — '

'No; there are other ways. Remember now — stay here until I return. Make yourself comfortable.'

Then Carter had vanished. He entered the library of the new wing a moment or two later, and Dr. Hargraves looked at him expectantly.

'Yes, I think I can manage it for you,' Carter said. 'I propose the identical routine — the changing of water into ice; the steel cube through the steel plate; and the bending aside of light-waves by mental polarization.'

'Excellent!' Hargraves shook hands warmly. 'I do thank you most sincerely, Mr. Bradman. I'll see to it that the press is well represented. Thank you again.'

And with much hand-shaking Hargraves went on his way and was shown out by Peters. Carter smiled a little to himself and then wandered into the drawing room where Vera was still lounging and reading.

'What did he want?' she asked languidly, and Carter told her. At which she sat up and looked at him.

'But, Harvey, how do you do such things? Are they really scientific miracles or just very clever conjuring tricks?'

'You don't deceive men like Dr. Hargraves with conjuring tricks, my dear! No, the whole thing is scientifically exact. It is the process of thought disturbances setting at naught the laws of physics.'

'Tell me more! This is the first time you've given me credit for having the intelligence to understand you.'

Carter sat down in the armchair Harvey had been using, and relaxed.

'I don't propose to go into a long winded explanation of control of thought-processes, Vee. I just couldn't cram years of knowledge into a few minutes.'

'Then let's talk about something else you understand. How about interplanetary travel? That always seems to have intrigued you — and it certainly intrigues me. It surprises me that since you have such a grasp of metaphysical mechanics you don't produce an easier way to cross space than by using expensive — and dangerous — rockets.'

'Oh, I have,' Carter responded, somewhat amusedly.

'Then why doesn't everybody know about it? Look, Harvey, there's no use you making great discoveries and then keeping them to yourself! Safer space travel is the one thing every scientist wants to get perfected, and you say you've done it?'

'I have, yes — but there are reasons at the moment why I don't reveal the facts.'

'Well I can't think of any good ones! Please, Harvey, tell me just a little — '

Carter smiled and rose to his feet. 'Some other time, Vee. Now excuse me for a moment or two, will you? I have some notes to look up in readiness for tomorrow night.'

He left the drawing room and returned quickly down the corridors to his own regions. Harvey was waiting impatiently.

'I accepted Hargraves' offer,' Carter said, closing the door, 'and so I'll perform for you tomorrow night. In case we don't meet before then, be here at about six-thirty and we will change places.'

'Okay,' Harvey assented brusquely, and headed for the door.

'And I hope you don't get too tied up with your wife, Mr. Bradman,' Carter added, chuckling. 'I've been having a few words with her — scientific words.'

'The devil you have!'

'I have left one or two scientific issues unanswered as far as your wife is concerned. Take care how you go if she persists in questioning you.'

Harvey gave a grunt of annoyance and returned to the drawing room. It appeared to him, from the way Vera was walking to the divan, that she too had been absent from the room. She had — as her next words revealed.

'You may try and hide your great discovery from me,' she said, 'but I'm determined you shan't hide it from the world. I've just phoned the boys of the press: they'll ferret the facts out of you.'

'And what am I supposed to be hiding?'

Vera stared. 'You know full well! A new method of space travel that makes rockets obsolete! You know how it can be done, you say, yet for some obscure reason you refuse to give science the benefit of your knowledge.'

'Oh,' Harvey said uneasily, and sat in the armchair. 'Well — er — that's because I think it might prove dangerous in inexperienced hands.'

'I don't call the expert scientists inexperienced, Harvey! That's no excuse — especially as you said your discovery was safer than rockets!'

'Mmmm,' Harvey mumbled, and contemplated the thought of dashing out to Carter for aid. Then it occurred to him this might not be forthcoming. Carter, evidently, had frozen up on information, and that in turn presented to Harvey another puzzle. Just why had Carter withheld the secret of one of the most burning problems of the day?

'Since you won't discuss space travel, nor detail in full your control over matter, what else have you got?' Vera asked, settling on the divan again. 'I don't quite like being treated as though I'm a child, you know.'

'Sorry,' Harvey apologized, still wondering if he was making the right moves in the right order. 'It isn't that I underrate your intelligence: it's just that there aren't the right words to convey my meaning adequately.'

Vera looked at him vaguely and he cleared his throat; then to prevent her questioning him further he began to make notes, taking care at the same time to make them undecipherable.

5

The apparition

When the gentlemen of the press arrived later that day Harvey had quite the most uncomfortable time of his life trying to explain away why he would not answer their questions. From him they could not extract a single scientific observation — which was not particularly surprising — yet this was the 'same man' who on the morrow was going to make matter turn somersaults. It was something the hard-boiled boys could not understand.

The result of the interviewing tornado left Harvey still pondering about space travel and at the back of his mind something was commencing to turn over. He was not quite sure yet what it was. The major fact looming was that Carter knew all about space travel because he had come from Procyon. The contributory fact was that every scientist on Earth was looking for a foolproof way of traversing space without recourse to rockets and recoil principles. If he, Harvey, could find such a secret — or more correctly steal it — then he might feel he amounted to something in his own right. So the thoughts turned over and gradually gathered more urgency.

Vera was definitely annoyed by his refusal to speak to the press. She felt her genius of a playboy scientist had let her down, particularly after the build-up she had given over the telephone. However, she consoled herself with the thought that Harvey would probably amply justify himself at the conference the following evening.

In the midst of these happenings Peters moved with silent efficiency, never missing a cue on either side of the house. His only diversion was to 'phone the London papers the details of staff advertisements and then pray that nobody would answer them!

Harvey for his part spent the day — except for meals — in the library, supposedly meditating on metaphysical power before his task in the evening. Vera saw little difference in his appearance after his efforts, but there definitely was a faint aroma of brandy around him. Just how the spirit of the playboy could so completely combine with the metaphysical scientist was something quite beyond her.

At six-thirty Harvey excused himself for a moment from the drawing room, and Carter reappeared in his place with the announcement that he was going to dress in preparation for his demonstration. Vera took it as a signal for her to dress as well since she definitely meant going with her husband to see him perform, whether she had been invited or not.

Meantime, Harvey was mooning around the old lounge and thinking all kinds of things to himself. It was a relief to him when towards seven-fifteen Peters appeared, bearing dinner.

'I thought, sir, I might as well attend to you as I would have done to Dr. Carter in the normal course of routine,' Peters explained. 'He has gone now, and madam has gone with him.'

'What!' Harvey exclaimed, getting out of the armchair.

Peters laid the table methodically. 'I was under the impression that that was part of the plan, sir.'

'Nothing of the kind! And I don't like Carter wandering around with my wife! That isn't in the bargain.'

Peters gave a dry smile. 'I am afraid a lot of things are not in the bargain, sir. Not that you need have any fear for madam, I am sure. Since Dr. Carter is a self-admitted denizen of another planet there can certainly be no single physical characteristic about your wife that can appeal to him. We are not dealing with a man, sir, but with — er — a creature.'

'And what a creature!' Harvey sat down at the table and frowned. 'You know, Peters, the main thing about him which puzzles me is how he knows exactly what is going on in the other wing. He couldn't possibly get all the details so pat from thought-reading alone.'

'No, sir. The explanation is comparatively simple — and after you have had your dinner I will, with your permission, show you something very interesting.'

'Good man!' Harvey enthused. 'And how comes it that you know so much about it?'

'I have kept track of our guest almost constantly, sir.' Peters was still calmly setting forth the meal from the dinner wagon. 'Indeed I have little else to do between times and, being so thoroughly conversant with the — hmm — layout of this building I can watch from places which our guest has yet to discover.'

Harvey nodded, all curiosity — but at the moment hunger had a greater claim so he tackled his meal. The moment he had finished, however, he submitted himself to Peters' guidance and found himself directed into the basement. His surprise was complete when the snap of a switch in the darkness brought electric light into being.

'I thought there was no power down here,' he remarked.

'There wasn't until Dr. Carter brought a generator, sir. It is in the next basement section — small but very efficient and constantly running. Maybe you can hear it?'

Harvey listened to the faint, distant hum and then nodded.

'I gather our guest means to equip his drawing room — or lounge — with electricity later,' Peters added. 'As yet he has not got around to it. Indeed he has spent a good deal of time painting over the windows of the rooms he uses in the old wing, so no light can be seen outside.'

'Charming fellow,' Harvey muttered, and still followed Peters, finally coming into a small off-cellar. Here the electric light was still in evidence, its brilliance casting upon equipment that was obviously of a radio-television nature.

'On one occasion recently,' Peters explained, 'I crept down here to see what our friend was up to. I found that on this screen was mirrored the drawing room in the new wing, and by the control of a simple-looking tuning device Dr. Carter was able to change the view to any room in the house. I assume the subsidiary loudspeaker here carries synchronized sound. More plainly, by this unique device — which would be a boon to our defence forces if we understood it, sir — he is able to see and hear everything that goes on.'

'So that explains it,' Harvey sighed. 'The man's far too deep for us, Peters. Anything else?'

'Not that we can readily understand, sir. You may be interested in the equipment in the next main cellar. It is not yet properly linked up, I fancy. Deliveries of more machines are awaited, as you know.'

Harvey nodded and with Peters at his side wandered into the next brightly lighted area. There was a considerable quantity of electric equipment here, but none of it made much sense at the moment. The most dominant object seemed to be a horizontal tube, completely transparent, and resting on a cradle. It was sealed except for one end where there was a chrome metal cap like an airlock. On the interior base of the tube was softly sprung leather and felt. Its length was about six feet and, at the moment, it was completely devoid of connections even though switchboards had been bedded down in the concrete close beside it.

'Any ideas, Peters?' Harvey glanced at the manservant.

'I'm afraid not, sir. It looks like a vacuum tube of some kind but its purpose defeats me. I am also defeated by the nature of this, which I noticed before when I dared to explore down here.'

Harvey moved over to another transparent cylinder, upright this time and not particularly large. Inside it was a queer grey-shaped plasma. An electric current was evidently passing through it for it surged and eddied mysteriously as the two men looked at it.

'Nasty looking stuff,' Harvey admitted. 'And I've no more idea than you what it is supposed to be.' He glanced around him. 'I wish to heaven I could fathom what this alien devil is getting at. He talks casually of experimenting, but it's the nature of the experiment which has me worried.'

Peters sighed. 'Whatever it may be, sir, there's nothing we can do about it.'

'Don't be too sure,' Harvey replied slowly. 'I've had an idea buzzing around now for some time which might rid us of our annoying guest.'

'Indeed, sir?'

'I'm thinking of a spaceship,' Harvey explained. 'If I could only find out how space can be travelled — in the way Carter travelled it, I mean — and could then decoy him into a projectile and fire him into the void so he could never get back, all our troubles would be over!'

Peters smiled rather sadly. 'You neglect many factors, sir. If you could find the secret and had such a space projectile built you would first be unable to decoy our friend because he would read your thoughts; and second, there would be no way of stopping him returning here even if you managed to get rid of him in the first place. Some kind of remote radio control would have to be used to keep the space machine from returning. Not very practical, sir, unfortunately.'

'I'll go on thinking about it just the same. Do you suppose that Carter has his

134

space travel formula written down some-where?'

'No idea, sir. That would depend upon its nature. If it is complicated then he probably has it recorded somewhere: if simple then he doubtless carries it in that unusual mind of his.'

Harvey was looking at the horizontal tube. 'You don't think that might be a space projectile, do you?'

'I don't think so, sir, unless a driving force has yet to be supplied. Concerning the possible space travel formula — maybe we could find something if we searched Dr. Carter's quarters. He is using quite a few rooms for various purposes.'

'Okay, let's take a look.'

'Incidentally, sir,' Peters continued, 'there are more ways of being rid of Dr. Carter than the complicated one of trying to hurl him into space. For instance he might . . . vanish!'

'What! You mean murder him?'

'I was loath to use the actual word, sir, but I am afraid that is what I do mean. Only if necessity demands it, that is, such as our own lives being in danger, for I would not put anything past Dr. Carter. If he were to vanish,' Peters continued calmly, 'there would be no proof of it whatsoever. He is supposed to be you, and nobody save you and I know any different. So — well, there it is.'

'Too gruesome, Peters. If I get rid of him at all I want to give him a chance to go on living, but not on this world. However, thanks for the tip.'

'There is also another point, sir. If you dispose of him you throw away all possibility of maintaining your reputation. Had you thought of that?'

'I had, yes. If I get rid of him I shall announce to the media that I have decided to retire from scientific work: that ought to let me out.'

'Yes, sir.' Peters did not sound too convinced. 'Let us hope so, sir.'

By this time they had regained Carter's rooms in the upper regions and, as before, Peters was still the guide. The rooms that Carter had commandeered, variously in use as drawing room, study, bedroom, and so forth were all examined carefully and the drawers investigated. Indeed none of the drawers or cupboards were locked — but nothing suggestive of a formula, or anything scientific at all, came to light. At last Harvey gave a sigh of disappointment.

'Looks as though you were right, Peters. The only place we'll find what we want is in Carter's mind — and that presents a man-sized difficulty!'

'Undoubtedly so, sir. We shall have to leave the matter for the time being and see if we have any better luck later.'

With that he cleared the remains of the dinner onto the wagon, Harvey watching him moodily.

'Did Carter say what time he would be back, Peters?'

'He gave no indication, sir.'

'Then I'll have to stop here until he shows up. You'd better stay in your normal regions in case you're caught out.'

'Very good, sir.'

So, until nearly midnight, Harvey lounged around, pondering, drinking, then lounging again — until at last there was a click at the door latch and Carter came in, removing his black overcoat and white scarf.

'Here,' he said, handing them over, 'hurry up and take my place. I escaped with a very vague excuse about checking something in the library.'

Harvey glanced down at his own evening dress, took the coat and scarf, then headed for the door.

'Where's the hat?' he asked.

'Peters took that. You gave a great performance tonight, Mr. Bradman. The papers will carry the full story tomorrow.'

Harvey departed and sped through the corridors, just coming into the hall as Vera also appeared from the staircase. She had evidently been upstairs to be rid of her cape. She looked at Harvey in some curiosity.

'You're looking hot and bothered, Harvey. Anything the matter?'

'No, no. Why should there be? Everything's fine! Peters fixed up any supper for us yet?'

'He's doing it now. Stop running about so much, and let's refresh.'

Harvey removed his coat and scarf and

then followed Vera into the lounge. Peters gave a vague look of relief.

'Thanks, Peters, that's all,' Harvey said. 'You can lock up and retire.'

'Yes, sir. Oh, might I enquire if you gave a successful demonstration tonight?'

Harvey gave a hurt glance from under his eyes, but Vera took up the thread — as Peters had guessed she would.

'He was superb, Peters! I still don't know how he did it and neither did the big-shot scientists who watched him. To me it was like a dream to watch him. So difficult to reconcile it with his playboy alias.'

'Yes, madam, I am sure. Would I be presumptive if I asked what specific feats were performed?'

'Over to you, Harvey,' Vera said, but he shook his head.

'Modesty forbids, Peters.'

'Modesty, with what he can do!' Vera exclaimed, nibbling at a sandwich. 'He froze water by looking at it, lighted a piece of wood by the same process, pushed metal through glass without breaking it — Oh, a host of things. Next time I must try and arrange it so that you can be present too, Peters.'

'Thank you, madam, that would be delightful. Good night, madam. Sir.'

Peters went, one sly eye peeping at Harvey. Harvey went on munching and passed no comment.

'Why so dull?' Vera asked at length.

'Not dull, dear. Just exhausted after my efforts. It's past midnight anyway. Let's get to bed, shall we?'

★   ★   ★

The papers the following morning devoted several columns to eulogizing Harvey's scientific powers. He was hailed as the greatest brain of the modern era, a master of metaphysics, and heaven knew what else. But now the papers were commencing to ask questions, and the one least likely to be able to answer them was Harvey.

When, asked the *Daily Reporter*, was the playboy-cum-wizard going to stop amusing himself and the public and give something worthwhile to science? Other newspapers asked even more open questions. With such scientific knowledge why could not Harvey Bradman use his vast wealth for the development of his ideas? Why not turn his talents to the destruction of fatal diseases, to the banishment of pain, to the cure of the insane? Why not perfect space travel, eliminate war, invent safety methods so that no train, airplane, or road vehicle could ever have an accident? Demonstrations were all very well, but something more concrete was needed.

'This,' Harvey said at breakfast, when he read what 'he' had done the previous night, 'is mainly your fault, my dear. If you hadn't told the boys of the press about my knowing the secret of revolutionary space travel there wouldn't have been all this hullabaloo!'

'I'm entirely in favour of it,' Vera answered flatly. 'No man with your talents should keep things to himself. Besides, I want to see your name on the scroll of science along with the great benefactors of the human race, the — '

'Begging your pardon, sir,' Peters' voice

suddenly interrupted, 'but the balance of the machinery has arrived.'

Harvey frowned. 'Machinery? What machinery?'

Peters grimaced and jerked his head slightly. Vera watched him in amazement.

'Peters, whatever is the matter with you?'

'Oh, I — er — beg your pardon, madam. Just a slight nervous trouble. It seems to be getting rather worse.'

'You should see a doctor, Peters.'

'Yes, madam, the thought had occurred to me — '

'Machinery!' Harvey gasped abruptly, jumping up. 'Why yes, of course! I'd forgotten all about it. Be back in a moment dear.'

He hurtled out of the room and Peters cleared his throat slightly. Vera frowned to herself, rose, and then strolled to the window overlooking the drive. Out there, blocking the view, were two enormous six-wheel lorries loaded with equipment from which tarpaulins were being dragged by half a dozen burly workmen. Harvey was also out there — or so it appeared.

Actually Harvey was biting his nails in Carter's lounge, having made a lightning switch. Carter, by reason of his television eye system, was in exactly the right clothes.

'What in the world Harvey wants with all that stuff is quite beyond me,' Vera muttered, half to herself.

'Some scientific experiment he has in mind, madam, I understand,' Peters commented.

'I'll take a closer look,' Vera decided — and there was nothing Peters could do to stop her. She went out into the driveway and Carter gave a grim glance as he saw her approaching.

'Better get back inside, Vee,' he said brusquely. 'You may be in the way. This stuff has to be manhandled into the basement by the central ramp.'

'That doesn't prevent me watching, does it? And I don't like being told I might be in the way, either! Whatever you do concerns me, doesn't it?'

'Yes, dear — within limits,' and with that Carter did not take any further notice of her, hoping to tire her out. But in that he misjudged her nature. She remained tenaciously, watching every detail, until finally the queerly designed equipment had been bedded down in the basement. Only then did the workmen depart and Vera looked about her curiously.

'Harvey, for the love of heaven, what is all this stuff for?'

'Top secret, Vee. You'll learn soon enough. Now let's get back into the house. I need a wash.'

To this Vera raised no objections. Carter steered her into the lounge, excused himself, and then fled into his own regions. Ten seconds later Harvey slowed in his run and ambled into the lounge. He found Vera gazing through the window.

'How quick you've been!' she exclaimed, turning. 'All that dust removed so soon! Did you use metaphysical processes?'

Harvey merely glanced and muttered something under his breath; then Vera's next words stopped him in his slow drift towards the divan. She was looking out of the window again, studying something intently.

'Harvey, there's something I don't quite understand.'

'Oh?' Harvey tried to sound casual. Perhaps something had slipped up somewhere after all.

'I can't make out why there is smoke coming from the main chimney stack of the old wing. Have you got a fire in one of the basements? I didn't notice it.'

'There's an incinerator,' Harvey answered — quite truthfully as it happened. 'I — er — pushed some rubbish in it. Packing and such like. It must have burned up.'

'Must have, yes. Seems to be burning the dickens of a time.'

'Damn Carter and his lounge fire,' Harvey muttered to himself; then steering his way around the divan he went to the bell-rope and tugged it. Meantime he scribbled a brief note, handing it to Peters as he entered. The signs Harvey gave were quite sufficient and a glance at the note made Peters start slightly. It said: PUT YOUR INFERNAL FIRE OUT!

'Oh, Peters,' Harvey said out loud, as Vera turned from the window, 'you had better serve lunch. I assume you held it up until I had finished in the basement?'

'Exactly so, sir. Everything is ready.'

Harvey jerked his head and Peters vanished quickly, on his way with the note to Carter — but he was back on duty again just in time as lunch commenced. A thought seemed to strike Vera as she ate.

'Peters, when did the newspapers say they would print the advertisements for staff which you gave them?'

'About ten days, madam. Space shortage, I understand.'

'Ten days! They could surely do better than that!'

They most certainly could — but Peters did not wish them to.

'Just have to manage as best we can for the time being,' Harvey said shrugging, which observation was met with an icy stare.

'If you'd spend less time playing about and frittering away your fortune on machinery, and instead produce something scientifically useful to clean the place up, the better I'd like it!'

'Can't be done, Vee. My mind's above such things.'

'Then it's no right to be — and I'm telling you straight that unless you justify yourself somehow and give the world some scientific invention there may be trouble. The papers are already showing their claws and they can make or break you.'

Harvey frowned to himself, and throughout the remainder of lunch he seemed to be thinking things over. The moment he had the chance to escape without seeming suspicious he did so — and inevitably finished up in Carter's quarters. Carter however, was in the basement and it was there that Harvey finally discovered him. He was busy testing his peculiar equipment, also having half an eye to the intertelevisor screen that mirrored Vera at the moment, reclining in an armchair and glancing through a woman's magazine.

'By rights,' Carter said, before Harvey could speak. 'I don't like you in this basement, but I suppose it can't be helped. You haven't the brains anyway to understand the equipment. Oh, and thanks for the note concerning the lounge fire. I'd overlooked the matter of fire. I'll arrange radiant heat henceforth, entirely invisible.'

'Arrange what you like,' Harvey answered, 'but for heaven's sake give me a break. The morning newspapers are demanding that I justify my reputation by giving something definite to the world. Vera too is pestering me that way — '

'I heard her.'

'Very well then. What about giving me something useful? Let's say the secret of safer space travel. You as good as told my wife that you have all the details. Pass them on to me and let me splash them as my own discovery.'

'And allow a lot of crack-brained fools with their power-complexed minds to take their weapons into space to wreak havoc? Oh no, Mr. Bradman!'

'Something else, then,' Harvey entreated.

Carter made a tiresome movement away from his machinery.

'Oh very well, then: I suppose I owe you something. You might try this.' He went to one of the instruments and to Harvey's surprise the front of it opened abruptly. In other words, what looked to be a perfectly smooth pillar of metal with a queer instrument on its summit was actually a safe as well with a brilliantly concealed door. Carter looked through a stack of notes and then brought a particular bundle of papers to light.

'Enjoy yourself with this,' he said, handing it over and re-closing the 'safe' door. 'I drafted it — and some other plans — in English, in case I should need to have them constructed at some future time. Any engineering firm will be able to manufacture it.'

'What is it?' Harvey asked, puzzling over the queer design and masses of equations.

'It is a magnetic levitator. By its use enormous weights can be lifted with the mere touch of a button on the instrument. A whole skyscraper could be raised, moved, and put down elsewhere without any trouble at all. Cars could be lifted into racks to save parking space — there are all manner of possibilities. Claim it as your own: it's one of my less ambitious efforts.'

Harvey looked in amazement. 'But

— how does it work? I've got to have some idea.'

'It utilizes Earth's — or any planet's — lines of force. By that machine which is fully detailed in those plans the lines of force, which are the outcome of gravity, can be 'dampened' down in any particular spot so that gravity loses its pull. After that directional beams can move the object so 'degravitated.' It is ideal for surface work, but no use for space travel. But you can tell the world it is a by-product of space-travel.'

'Thanks,' Harvey said. 'Keep me going for a while anyway. Now I'll leave you to yourself again.'

Carter merely grunted and continued with the adjustments to his equipment. Harvey glanced at Vera on the screen, and then he made his way back to his own regions. But he did not join Vera. Instead he peeped in at the kitchen and motioned to Peters.

'Yes, sir?' Peters asked, coming out into the passageway.

Harvey jerked his head and, puzzled, Peters followed his master into the big yard at the rear of the modern wing.

'Just precaution,' Harvey explained. 'I don't think Carter will be able to overhear us out here: in fact I'm sure of it. Anyway, the point is, I've found his safe!'

'You have, sir? My heartiest congratulations.'

'I kept my thoughts as vague as possible in case he guessed I have designs on that safe,' Harvey continued. 'And I most certainly have. Amongst the papers he's got piled in it there may be space travel secrets, to say nothing of other immensely valuable formulae. Even this in my hand here, which he calls second-rate, is far ahead of anything we've developed as yet. As you can see, it's written in English, so that Earth engineers could construct it. I assume his other papers are the same.'

Peters looked puzzled, so Harvey gave every detail of what had been transpiring.

'Excellent, sir,' Peters said finally. 'I assume then that you will give the details of this levitator to the world and call it your own?'

'Exactly. Since I haven't the foggiest idea how it works I will let Dr. Hargraves have it. He'll do the rest and praise me to the skies. You see, Peters, we're ready now to make a plunge,' Harvey went on earnestly. 'I have established myself as a scientist, and given this levitator to the world: on the strength of that alone I could retire from scientific activity and . . . dispose of Carter. I'm prepared to make the attempt, anyway. He's up to something very grandiose in that basement and I think he'd be safer out of the way.'

'I agree, sir. What then is the next move?'

'There are two moves. First I send this invention to Dr. Hargraves, and second we try and investigate that safe tonight. Since it would be dangerous to appropriate whatever we may discover I propose to photograph it instead. I want you to get on the move right away. Take this material to Dr. Hargraves, and also call on our friend Mr. Danvers, the photographer, and buy a first class micro-camera from him, together with the necessary flashes and what-have-you.'

'I understand, sir. I will make ready immediately.'

Harvey nodded, handed over the bundle of notes, and then returned into the house with Peters behind him. Entering the lounge Harvey gave Vera a superior glance.

'For your information, my dear,' he said, casually inspecting his fingers. 'I have dashed off a little idea that may revolutionize all normal ways of levitating things.'

Vera laid aside her magazine. 'Levitating things? Hasn't that something to do with Yogi?'

'Certainly not!' Harvey snapped irritably. 'In the scientific sense it refers to things like cranes, elevators, weight-lifting apparatus, and so forth. I've sent Peters off with a notion that will first startle Dr. Hargraves, and then the world. And for the moment it is all I am going to give.'

'Yet you still remain cagey about revolutionary space travel?'

'Definitely I do. I still haven't got it perfect and an imperfect invention would smash my reputation to bits.'

So Vera said no more and Harvey at least felt he was entitled to some peace for a while. He got it, spending the rest of the afternoon supposedly making important notes, but all the time wondering what the blazes was really going on in the basement. Vera was wondering the same thing, from a different angle, and after dinner that evening she brought the matter up.

'Just what use is all that machinery you got, Harvey, if you don't get some work done with it?'

Harvey flourished the bundle of valueless papers upon which he was still scribbling. 'These are my preliminary notes, Vee. I've got to be absolutely sure of what I'm doing before I start work with that stuff.'

Vera sighed and got to her feet. 'I find life pretty boring here, Harvey. More so than I ever thought it would be. You spend all your time making notes and disappearing on mysterious errands. Why can't we go into town?'

'Tonight?'

'What's wrong with it? It's only quarter to nine.'

Harvey shook his head. 'Sorry, dear. You married a scientist first and playboy second. I've simply got to detail this plan of action so I can start work with my equipment tomorrow.'

Vera shrugged and moved around restlessly. 'I'll ask some of the gang over for the weekend if you don't mind. Break things up a bit. Won't interfere with your experiments, will it?'

'Shouldn't do.' And Harvey again lost himself in 'meditation' to avoid further questioning. It was an attitude he managed to maintain until bedtime — bar a few drinks and a visit to Peters in the kitchen to fix the time for 'exploration' of the basement.

And so to bed — at least as far as Vera and Harvey were concerned. Peters did not retire. Knowing the layout of the building so intimately he was keeping watch for the moment when Carter too would retire, and it proved to be towards three before he deserted his mysterious work in the basement and made his way to his bedroom. But Peters still waited, until at last it was four o'clock — then he glided back into the modern wing and finally reached the corridor alcove where Harvey was waiting for him.

'Where in the world have you been?' Harvey whispered. 'You said three o'clock.'

'Yes, sir — and my apologies. I have been waiting for Dr. Carter to get to sleep. I fancy the coast is now clear. Pardon me a moment.'

Peters vanished in the intense gloom and returned after a while with a rucksack over his shoulder. From it he unloaded torches, two new automatics, the micro-camera and flashbulbs, and one or two common-or-garden tools, which might prove helpful in safecracking.

'Everything the doctor ordered,' Harvey murmured. 'Good man! Let's be on our way. I don't like the idea of the guns, though,' he added, putting one of the automatics in his pocket.

'Possibly not, sir, but Dr. Carter might stop at nothing if he finds us invading his domain. In that case we'll have no alternative but to shoot him. I trust madam is sound asleep?'

'Definitely,' Harvey replied, and moved forward like a shadow.

Reaching the basement regions was not particularly difficult nor had Carter tried to lock the door that led to below. In perfect silence the two men crept down into the curious musty warmth. It was plain from the deadening odor of chemicals and latent heat in the air that Carter had done plenty of mysterious work before retiring.

'I suppose we daren't switch on the lights?' Harvey asked, listening to the distant faint humming of the generator

'I wouldn't recommend it, sir. Our torches should be adequate, granting you know the position of the safe.'

'Sure thing.'

Harvey switched on his torch and the beam cast around on the massive equipment, presently settling on the pillar, which looked as though it were supporting an instrument.

'Is that it?' Peters asked, surprised.

'Uh-huh. Cunning, isn't it? Whether we'll be able to open it or not I don't know.'

They came level with the pillar's smooth surface and could only just detect the thin hairline oblong, which marked the door. There was no visible catch, no knob to pull upon — just the smooth metal.

'Possibly a hidden spring, sir.' Peters said, feeling around on the metal — but thoroughly though he and Harvey investigated they could find no way of getting that door open.

'Perhaps a lock operated by thought-waves, sir,' Peters suggested at last. 'That would after all be the most foolproof method. If that should be so — '

He broke off, freezing at a sudden curious sound. It was rather like the hiss of air from a slow-punctured tire and was soon followed by the mysterious clicking of switches. Then varicolored lights began to flash around the laboratory. The two men remained motionless, their torch beams trying to pick up the source of the disturbances.

'It's — it's in that horizontal tube there,' Harvey panted, his beam directed that way. 'Something's moving inside it!'

'Yes, sir,' Peters confirmed, scared to death.

Neither of them felt capable of putting one foot before the other, so they remained by the pillar and watched the tube. From the chromium 'airlock' end something was sliding forward and at length it dropped to the floor. It was vaguely white and phantasmal in movement. Harvey's torch beam was wavering so much it was impossible to be certain of the nature of the apparition.

Not that it mattered for the lights suddenly came on without any visible reason.

'Holy cats,' Harvey whispered, his voice choked. 'Do you see what I see?'

Peters certainly did, but he had no idea what to do about it. For now the 'apparition' that had come from the tube was picking itself up. It was no diabolical horror, no manifestation of the supernatural, but a woman. A magnificent woman, the almost diaphanous shroud being her only garment. The lights casting through it revealed every curve of her flawless figure and reflected back from her sweeping tresses of yellow hair. Definitely she was beautiful — uncannily beautiful in that not one feature was out of proportion.

'Re — remarkable, sir,' Peters commented thickly. 'A most delectable young lady.'

'And she came out of that tube!' Harvey added, then he sweated whilst he waited to see what happened next.

6

Synthetic woman

With movements that were a sheer symphony of grace the mystery woman glided towards Harvey, her large smoke-blue eyes fixed upon him. He clung hold of Peters desperately, but not for long. When she reached him the woman slid her arms about his neck and held him firmly, her exquisite face only a few inches from his own.

Harvey was vaguely conscious of the fact that she smelled of curiously sickly antiseptics, that her body was warm and alive — then he dragged himself free, pushing the woman's hands away from him.

'Out!' he gasped to Peters. 'Quickly!'

'Just as you say, sir — '

They fled for the staircase leading to the upper regions but just as they reached it there was a sound at the summit. They slowed, gazed up at the figure of Dr. Carter. He had a dressing gown thrown about his pyjamas and there was a curious expression upon his face. He looked half pleased and half astonished, but certainly not angry.

'So she lives!' he exclaimed, coming slowly down the steps. 'My beautiful Oena lives!'

'Definitely,' Harvey agreed; then it suddenly dawned on him that he and Peters had no right to be down here and he waited for the storm to break. Carter, however, did not appear particularly disturbed by the invasion of his scientific territory. He joined the two men at the base of the steps and then glanced again towards the woman. She was standing motionless, a little frown of bewilderment notching her flawless forehead.

'Who the devil is she, Carter?' Harvey demanded, tossing overboard all ideas about explaining his presence down here.

'She is mine,' Carter answered, clasping his hands in ecstasy. 'I created her — a combination of synthetic flesh and tissue, cosmic radiation, mitogenesis, and a patterner.'

'You mean you made her?' Peters gasped.

'Just so.' There was a dreamy look in Carter's eyes. 'I was not sure if the experiment would work, but obviously it has, magnificently! Out of plasma, which I formerly kept in an electrically controlled tube over there, I produced the basic ingredients. I then selected patterns from what I considered the most beautiful women on this planet — much as I patterned myself after you, Mr. Bradman — and so I formed the composite. All unknowingly, various women on this world have supplied the pattern of a body, a face, hair, and so forth — the best quality being selected from each. Ah, superb, is she not?'

'You did all this and just left her to sort of come to life?' Harvey asked, stumbling over the impossible situation.

'Hardly that. I carried the experiment as far as I could of my own accord and then left mechanical devices to do the rest. When she came to life fully formed I had it arranged for an alarm to sound in my bedroom. It did so, which brought me here. She, owing to the ordered impression on her synthetic brain, delivered herself from the creation-tube and in doing so her body intercepted an electromagnetic beam, which put up the laboratory lights. I contrived that so she would be able to see her surroundings and not destroy herself in sudden fear at the strangeness of her birth.'

'Would you mind telling me why you had to create this woman?' Harvey demanded. 'She may make things damned difficult for both of us.'

'Difficult? Oena?' Carter laughed scornfully. 'She will do only as she is told, my friends, nothing more. As to why I created her — I had to have a mate. As a single unit on this world my existence was becoming purposeless.'

'Aren't there plenty of women — normal ones — from whom you could have chosen?' Harvey asked, surprised.

'That presented difficulties, Mr. Bradman. For one thing I cannot leave here without involving you. For another — a much more important reason — there are no women on this planet worthy of mating with me. I am superior to all of them, as I am to you. Therefore I decided on the creation of a woman of the exact standard I require, not so much as an intellectual equal but as a companion and the first woman of a new race. In time we can found an empire for our progeny.'

'I think I see what you mean,' Peters said slowly. 'You have led me to think all along that you were simply an outcast, or survivor, from your own barren world and that you required sanctuary wherein to meditate and experiment. Now it becomes obvious you have used Mr. Bradman as a cover for your activities, your real aim being the establishment of your particular race, of which this woman is the prime agency. Put more simply you mean to bring a race into being and what happens to us, of this world, doesn't matter!'

'Correct,' Carter agreed calmly.

'If you can create life as easily as this why didn't you create a race that way?' Harvey questioned.

'Because there are not enough basic materials. From this world's basic elements I succeeded in deriving just enough to form the body of this woman. The rest will be normal procreation. Yes, Mr. Bradman, I have used you as a cover, letting you trump up your silly little personality into something great whilst I have been engaged on this. I am prepared to continue as your scientific shadow for many years until my great experiment, which has begun here, reaches fruition. And you cannot stop me because I can always read what you are thinking.'

There was silence. During the conversation the woman had glided nearer. Now, ignoring Carter completely, she again put her soft arms about Harvey's neck and drew him gently towards her. Before he realized what had happened she had kissed him warmly.

'Hey, wait a minute!' he insisted, doing his best to push her away, and as his efforts proved unavailing Peters raised an eyebrow and cleared his throat gently.

'This is very strange,' Carter mused, studying the woman's beautiful face.

'And embarrassing!' Harvey objected, still struggling. 'Get her away from me, can't you?'

'Go!' Carter commanded her, pointing imperiously; but the woman took no notice. She did, however, speak in a gentle, melodious voice.

'I obey only my creator. I cannot do aught else.'

'Eh?' Harvey looked into smoke-grey eyes with the languid black lashes curling over them. 'But — but I didn't create you. I wish you'd — '

'Mr. Bradman, something serious has happened,' Carter interrupted in consternation. 'I should have thought of it before. Order her away! Command her to sit on that chair over there.'

'Who? Me? Well, all right — Sit down over there, Oena,' Harvey ordered, and immediately the woman released him and moved with the grace of a panther to the chair he had indicated. She sat down, a creation of ineffable loveliness in her transparent shroud.

'Very interesting,' Carter remarked, thinking.

167

Harvey straightened his collar. 'For you maybe. I shudder to think what would happen if my wife had happened to come in at that moment. In fact I'm shuddering anyway. If this woman should escape — '

'I have made a grave mistake,' Carter cut in.

'That, sir, is an understatement,' Peters commented. 'Though I must confess the young lady, synthetic or otherwise, has a definite — hmm — attraction!'

'You make me sick,' Carter snapped. 'All you see is this woman's form and then lose your self control. All you males on this planet are alike! For me this woman is merely a means to an end — or at least she was. The trouble is, Mr. Bradman, you have ruined my entire experiment! What the devil do you and Peters mean by coming down here? You had no right!'

'This is my house and my basement,' Harvey retorted. 'That gives me all the right in the world. You don't even pay any rent, which might serve to make your territory more sacrosanct. And I haven't ruined your experiment, either! We came down here to find out what you were up to — and we did.'

'You are sure that is all you came for?' Carter's eyes were glinting as he obviously read Harvey's mind. 'It seems to me you came to steal some scientific secrets. You hoped to open that safe of mine. You can spare yourselves any trouble on that account. That safe is controlled by thought waves and only I know what those thought waves are. However, regarding my experiment, you have ruined it insofar that this woman believes you created her instead of me.'

'Why should she?'

'Because you were the first person on whom she set eyes, whereas it should have been me. Let me explain it to you in scientific terms. This woman has a brain, upon which — whilst I created her — I impressed certain thoughts. For one thing I gave her the language, and a complete awareness of bodily movement and coordination. I also gave her a mental impression of my own appearance and impressed upon her that I alone made her and that she must obey only me. I made it clear to her brain that the first person she would see upon coming to active life would be me — as I fully believed it would be. But instead you, my double, proved to be first. Her brain is so set that her impression cannot be reversed, therefore she believes you created her and she will obey only you and nobody else.'

'Well — er — can't you make adjustments?' Harvey demanded.

'That might be possible and I would have to think it out. In the meanwhile I can do nothing. You must deal with her as you deem best. If you destroy her I shall kill you, my friend. She is too valuable to lose.'

Harvey looked at Peters, but for once the manservant was at a loss.

'If I find I cannot possibly adjust her brain so that she responds only to me, I shall have to remodel her,' Carter added finally. 'If you two fools hadn't meddled down here this would never have happened.'

Harvey cleared his throat. 'Well, she'll have to stay here for the time being for obvious reasons. Let's get out of here,

Peters, and see if we can think what comes next.'

'Very good, sir.'

Watched by Carter's malignant eyes, and the soulful gaze of the synthetic woman, Harvey fled for the stairs with Peters close behind him. They hurried up them and into the main corridor, gradually retracing their way through the gloom — until Harvey remembered he still had his torch in his pocket.

'This is a pretty mess, Peters,' he observed, when at last they had reached their own region of the great house.

'As you say, sir. I — er — find it somewhat hard to credit that the young lady below is purely a thrown-together mass of chemicals and synthetic flesh. Most attractive, sir — most.'

'You don't have to keep telling me that, do you? The point is how do we — Oh, Lord,' Harvey finished in dismay, as suddenly the lights came up in the passage and Vera came into view, her silken gown drawn together over her nightdress.

'So there you are!' she exclaimed,

coming forward. 'I've been looking everywhere for you; then I heard you talking. Just what are you doing? And with Peters too! I got the fright of my life when I found you'd vanished.'

'Fright?' Harvey tried to sound unconcerned. 'Why? I might have gone — er — well, anywhere!'

'That's what I mean. A scientist who can do what you can is likely to sideslip into the fourth dimension, or something, at any moment. Just what are you up to at this time of night? You too, Peters!'

'We've just been conducting an experiment, dear,' Harvey smiled. 'In the basement. No job for a woman to do otherwise I'd have asked you to help me.'

'That, madam, is certainly correct,' Peters confirmed.

Vera looked from one to the other, her loosened hair bobbing quite attractively about her shoulders.

'Anything to stop me seeing what you've done in the basement?' she asked abruptly.

'Well, I — I hardly think it would be advisable, dear.' Harvey took her arm gently. 'Great deal of static and free electrons down there. Wouldn't do you any good.'

He paused as Vera suddenly looked beyond him down the passage. Peters looked too and his expression was quite enough to make Harvey shut his eyes.

'Master — creator — why did you leave me?' There was no denying that voice, plaintive and inhumanly seductive.

'This,' Harvey whispered, 'is it!'

Vera did not appear to hear him. She was staring frozenly at the lightly clad woman coming down the passage in the bright electric lights. She moved, as before, like a phantom, yet every movement was uttermost grace.

'For the love of heaven, who's this?' Vera gasped at last, and her voice was a mere squeak. 'Harvey! Harvey, you fool! Get your eyes open — if you dare!'

Harvey looked, and gulped. That which happened next was the very thing he feared. Oena reached him, slid her arms about his neck, and kissed him. Then she remained holding him, her magnificent body pressed close against his. Vera watched, her eyes so wide they looked as though she would never blink again.

'It's — er — something I've been dabbling with,' Harvey explained desperately, trying to tug away from the twining arms. 'She isn't a real woman, dear — '

'What!' Vera screeched.

'I mean she's synthetic. Just made up of odd bits. Photographs re-imposed on flesh and then geared up into life.'

'Correct, madam,' Peters added, nervously plucking at his black tie.

'Be quiet, Peters! And I'm astounded to think that a sober man like you can have any connection with such — such utterly immoral goings-on!'

'Just a minute, this isn't immoral!' Harvey insisted. 'Oena is a perfectly nice girl — in so far as her synthetic limitations permit. Oena, release me!'

She obeyed immediately and stood with her hands at her sides. She was quite unabashed by the arctic stare Vera was directing upon her.

'As a scientist, Vee, I'm liable to do all sorts of things,' Harvey explained — or tried to. 'Don't you realize what a wonderful thing I have done? I've actually made a living being! A woman! It's never been done before.'

'Anything else?' Vera asked, in a faraway voice.

'She's purely for demonstration purposes, aren't you, Oena?'

'You made me,' she answered softly. 'You created me, moulded every line of my body and — '

'I see,' Vera interrupted. 'So this is the top secret, Harvey? This is the reason for scores of thousands of pounds worth of equipment! Or is it? Personally I consider you've used your scientific genius and so-called experiments as a blind to disguise your lust. Yes, lust! It's nothing else. You've had this half naked female hidden in the cellar all the time! No wonder you were always dashing off! No wonder you did not want me in the basement. Believe me, Harvey, I'll make such a row about this to the papers your head will sing for years afterwards!'

'But honestly, Vee — '

Vera was not listening. She swung on her heel and with a crisp rustle of silk went sweeping down the right-angled passage, which led to the hall and staircase.

'Hold onto Oena, Peters,' Harvey ordered, and went chasing after Vera as hard as he could go. Peters watched him go, then he caught at Oena's arm as she made to follow.

Be it said to Peters' credit that he intended to hold the synthetic woman by main force, but he had completely underestimated her astonishing strength. Carter had infused into her muscular structure something of the great power which he himself possessed: accordingly Oena tore free of Peters' grip, so violently indeed he twirled round and fell on his knees. In horror he watched that superb form racing away in the direction of the hall.

'Only one way out of this,' Peters muttered, and the thought was no sooner in his mind than he was racing back to Dr. Carter's quarters. He found him at last in the basement, figuring busily between intervals of gazing into space.

'Well, Peters, what is it?' he asked impatiently.

'If I may be forgiven, sir, there never was a time when your help was so urgently needed! Oena is on the rampage.'

'I know. I couldn't stop her. It's Mr. Bradman's fault.'

'Maybe it is, but if you don't watch out, sir, Mrs. Bradman will destroy that robot of yours. Kill it, or something. She is just in the mood — '

Carter's expression changed. He put down his notes and crossed to his inter-televisor. Switching it on he adjusted the control until a bedroom came in view. Vera was half clad, struggling into a dress. Nearby was Harvey waving his hands about desperately. In the open doorway, calmly watching, stood Oena, like something out of heaven.

Sound gushed suddenly in the speakers. ' . . . and that's the whole truth, Vee! You've got to believe me. At least let me have scientists examine Oena and prove she isn't a real woman but a carbon copy.'

'Examine her!' Vera twirled angrily. 'Harvey, how much further are you going to go? Look at her! Not even dressed

177

properly — I'm getting out, and you'll hear from my lawyer as soon as may be.'

Vera brushed past Harvey, buttoning up her dress savagely as she went. Reaching the wardrobe she dragged out a suitcase and threw it on the ottoman at the base of the bed. Oena began to move forward, her arms extended towards Harvey — and on that Carter switched off.

'Dangerous,' he admitted. 'Very dangerous. Mrs. Bradman might very easily do my robot irreparable damage if her temper gets out of control. I have been trying to devise ways of adjusting Oena's mind — '

'The only thing to save the situation is to take the master's place, sir,' Peters insisted. 'You have the power of mental compulsion to make her believe that Oena is only synthetic. Once that's done she'll accept the situation. It will also get Mr. Bradman out of a terrible mess.'

'I'm not thinking about that fool; I'm thinking of the robot,' Carter retorted, commencing to undress quickly. 'I'll do it anyway. Fetch me identical clothes to your master's.'

178

Peters nodded and hurried from the basement. In ten minutes of frantic arranging and checking Carter was ready and hurried to the upstairs, Peters behind him. When they had at last reached the region of the bedroom Carter paused, listening to Vera's angry voice.

' . . . and that's all, Harvey! You can keep your confounded double life and I'll expose you to the limit. Good bye!'

In the bedroom Harvey looked help-lessly at Vera's angry face. She had her outdoor clothes on and a packed suitcase. Oena was reclining against the bed, smiling gently towards her 'creator'. Then with a final glare Vera swung out of the room and marched down the passage. She had covered half a dozen yards when she realized she was again looking at Harvey, with Peters behind him.

'Surprised, dear?' Carter asked pleasantly. 'After all, I am a scientist of unusual gifts, remember, and I still insist that Oena is synthetic.'

'How — how did you — get here?' Vera's face was a study.

'Oh — hyper-spatial transit. I — '

It was no use talking to Vera any more. She had fainted, flat out. Carter looked down at her, then lifted her into his arms with superlative ease. Peters picked up the suitcase and so the unconscious Vera was brought back into the bedroom. Harvey gave a violent start when he saw what had happened.

'What does this mean?' he demanded, staring at Vera's recumbent form on the bed.

'I'm taking your place,' Carter told him. 'Your wife saw me immediately after you because I'd no chance to hide. The shock laid her low. Get down to my quarters and take Oena with you. I'll do the rest.'

'But what are you — '

'Hurry!' Carter snapped. 'Your wife may recover at any moment.'

Harvey clenched his fists and strode to the doorway.

'Oena, follow,' he ordered, and the synthetic woman glided happily after him. Peters, looking half dead from lack of sleep, waited for something else to happen. Indeed it was happening already

180

for Vera was slowly recovering. Finally, with Carter's arm behind her shoulders, she sat up.

'Better?' Carter smiled. 'You had a nasty turn, my dear. Some sort of delusion that suddenly got you. You raved about a synthetic woman, or something, swore you'd get a divorce, and then made to leave the house. It was then that you fainted.'

Vera did not comment. She looked at Peters and read nothing from his expression. Very gradually she assumed a sitting posture and seemed to be pondering.

'Anything I can get you, madam?' Peters asked politely.

Still Vera did not answer. Something seemed to be chasing around in her mind, which she could not pin down. Finally she looked at Carter steadily.

'There never was a synthetic woman, Harvey?'

'Course not, darling. Some silly dream or delusion that got you. Maybe radiations from the basement where Peters and I have been working.'

'I see. Help me off the bed, Harvey. I feel better now.'

Carter complied and, her feet on the floor again, Vera looked about her. Then she snapped: 'Where's Harvey?'

Carter looked surprised. 'But I'm here, dearest — '

'I'm talking to you, Peters! Where is my husband?'

Peters fluttered helplessly but could not find anything to say. Vera turned slowly to look at Carter. From his hard concentration of expression Peters judged that he was trying to read thoughts.

'For your benefit,' Vera said, 'whoever you may be, I was not entirely unconscious when I collapsed in the passage. I admit shock overcame me for a moment, that and reaction from the earlier experiences with that half dressed female from the basement. But I heard everything you said, and I heard my husband answer you! I gather he is somewhere in the house, so fetch him, Peters! I demand a showdown to all these crazy happenings.'

Carter relaxed slowly and gave a rather

grim smile. 'You have quite a gift for keeping your thoughts jumbled, Mrs. Bradman,' he commented. 'I certainly did not read in them that you had guessed the truth.'

'That's not surprising! I haven't guessed anything yet: I'm in a complete daze. But I do know you talked to my husband and that he had little chance to answer you. Who are you? His identical twin, or something?'

'You might call me that,' Carter admitted. 'I suppose it was bound to happen sooner or later — this exposure, I mean. Not that it makes any difference, of course, because my mind is superior to that of anybody on this planet.'

'You mean . . . ' Vera felt an icy little thrill pass through her, but she was self-possessed enough not to show it: then she looked towards the doorway as Harvey came hurrying in. Peters was right behind him, and — after a second or two — Oena sidled in softly too, catching at Harvey's arm.

'Hello, Vee,' Harvey said dully. 'Peters tells me you've tumbled to the truth.'

183

'That's just what I haven't done. Don't you think it's about time you explained yourself?'

'It'll mean the end of the scientific giant when I do. I'm just what I've always been — a gin drinking lounge lizard.'

'Oh, come on,' Vera insisted irritably. 'The facts, Harvey! The facts! What's all this about?'

So Harvey told her everything, from the very beginning. It took him nearly twenty minutes and Oena remained beside him throughout the period. At the end of it Vera was slumped in the basket-chair by the window, somewhat overpowered by the mixture of science and deception. Carter for his part was making notes on a piece of paper beside the bed, not at all concerned with the proceedings. As for Peters, he looked as if he were asleep standing up.

'So that's it,' Vera said at last, raising and lowering her hands helplessly. 'You've been trading on the name of this being from another planet. He has been you in the scientific moments — and at other times when I needed convincing. Very nice! Very pretty!'

'At least, madam,' Peters said, coming to life, 'it explains why the robot here is so attached to Mr. Bradman. Believe me, that is the absolute truth. Mr. Carter here cannot find a way to alter her brain, so — '

'I think I have a way,' Carter interrupted, rising. 'Let us get this situation into focus, shall we? The facts are now known to you, Mrs. Bradman, so your husband has no need to indulge in any more subterfuge. He can still retain his pose as a master scientist if he wishes: I will grant him what aid he may need.'

'That's the least you can do,' Vera said acidly.

'On the more personal side something must be clearly understood by all three of you,' Carter continued. 'Oena is my prospective mate, for the propagation of my race on this planet, and I am determined she shall fulfill the destiny for which I created her.'

'Which means you are aiming at starting your own race of supposedly more intelligent people and crushing us out?' Vera asked.

'The lesser always fall before the greater, Mrs. Bradman. That is inevitable law. However, in her present condition Oena cannot fulfill the function for which she was made because of her attachment to your husband. There is only one way to straighten out this situation — only one way whereby your husband will never be troubled with Oena again, only one way whereby I can claim Oena, as I intended in the first place.'

'And what's that?' Vera asked suspiciously.

'I must perform a brain operation on you, Mr. Bradman, and remove the section which is creating a mentally magnetic attraction for Oena. By altering that attraction I can make it so that Oena will be repulsed by you. After that, a slight adjustment to her own brain will turn her constantly to me. It is merely an elementary matter of brain surgery and re-arrangement of cells and ganglia.'

'Not if I know it!' Vera declared stoutly, jumping up. 'My husband has been messed about enough, with your confounded experiments. This is one time he won't obey.'

Harvey looked surprised. 'Well, Vee, thanks for sticking up for me! I thought after all that had happened you'd — '

'You've been a sponge-headed ninny all through, as usual, but you're my husband and I'll back you to the end against this monster! How do you like that, Mr. Procyon?'

Carter merely smiled. 'If you do not agree, Mr. Bradman, you will have Oena to explain away as long as you live. She will never grow old, remember.'

Harvey thought for a moment, then he said, 'This may surprise you, Carter — and you, Vee — but I'm prepared to undergo this brain surgery business.'

'What!' Vera gasped in horror.

'On one condition! In return I am to be given every scientific secret I desire, in order to build up and maintain my reputation as a supposed scientific wizard. I'm not losing my hold on that for anybody. So it's up to you now, Carter. You want Oena and I want to be rid of her. Give me what I'm asking for or you'll find things will stay just as they are.'

'Well!' Vera exclaimed in surprise. 'I do believe you have some business instincts after all, Harvey!'

Harvey did not answer. He was looking at Carter, and to judge from the expression on Carter's face he did not like the situation at all.

'Supposing I promised to grant your request, Mr. Bradman. How do you know I would keep my word after operating upon you?'

'I'd make sure of the formulae you gave me before the operation, believe me! And you won't be able to hand me bundles of worthless notes, either, relying upon my ignorance. I shall submit everything you give me to Dr. Hargraves, one of the best scientists in the world, and if he approves them — as he already has my levitator — then I'm ready for you to begin.'

'I see,' Carter said gravely. 'Which means you have driven me into quite a corner, Mr. Bradman. Not that it can make much difference in the long run, however. Very well. I accept your proposition. What secrets do you want?'

'Your new form of space travelling, and inter-television.'

Carter hesitated; then he shrugged. 'Very well. I'll get the necessary formulae and specifications from my basement safe. But I'm withholding the secret of hyper-spatial transit for faster than light travel: the space machine design I shall give you shall be limited to travelling in your own solar system. Your engineers couldn't construct an interstellar drive anyway . . . In the meantime something has to be done to keep Oena away from you.'

'I would suggest taking her into the basement and locking her in a cupboard or something,' Harvey suggested. 'I'll get her there; then you, Carter, can see that she does not escape until such time as the operation on me begins.'

'Agreed,' Carter assented.

Harvey turned to the synthetic woman. 'Come with me, Oena. We shall have to be parted for a while. And, Dr. Carter, I'll thank you, after giving me the formulae I want, to remain in your own part of the house until we make fresh arrangements. Even though my wife is now fully aware of what is going on I don't wish you mixing with us.'

'I have no desire to,' Carter replied coldly. 'Shall we go?'

7

The space machine

It was breakfast time when at last Harvey had looked through the various formulae and designs, which Carter had grudgingly given him. Vera, looking somewhat washed out after the disturbed night — and Peters doing his best to stifle yawns — looked at Harvey expectantly as he came over to begin his meal.

'Think the stuff he's given you is genuine?' Vera asked.

'For myself I can't say: I'm no scientist. Hargraves will answer that one. I'm going to see him immediately after breakfast and if everything's all right, that's that.'

'I still don't like it.' Vera took a drink of her coffee. 'He could kill you during that brain operation — and, as he feels at the moment, probably will.'

'No, he can't do that.' Harvey shook his head. 'He has to alter my brain to somehow make me mentally repulse Oena. That just couldn't be obtained if I were dead. Then she'd probably be grief stricken, and still wouldn't be attracted to him.'

'And when the operation is over, sir, will that be the end of the story?' Peters enquired. 'After that will Dr. Carter be allowed to continue just as he chooses until at length with the passage of years, humanity starts to come under his shadow?'

Instead of answering Harvey wrote a brief note and showed it first to his wife, then to Peters. It read: THIS ROOM IS WIRED UP FOR SOUND, REMEMBER. I'LL EXPLAIN EVERYTHING LATER.

'Can I come with you to London?' Vera asked. 'I don't like the idea of being left with only Peters to protect me from that monster.'

'Yes, you're coming with me,' Harvey assented. 'You had better come as well, Peters. If Carter has the run of the house whilst we're gone it doesn't make any difference.'

So it was decided, and shortly after ten o'clock, Harvey set off in his powerful racer. Vera sat beside him and Peters in the rear seat. The moment the drive was well under way Harvey began talking.

'Out here we can talk freely without the risk of being overheard,' he said. 'You may remember, Peters, that I once had an idea about firing our annoying friend into space and trapping him there so he could never come back to Earth?'

'I recall the notion clearly, sir,' Peters agreed, a hand on his bowler hat as the wind sought to snatch it away.

'If amongst these formulae there is a genuine space-travelling method I'm going to try that plan out — and make Oena the means of making it work. Carter thinks himself so superior to everybody else it would be a decided shock if the gin-sodden playboy beat him to it in the finish, wouldn't it?'

'You really believe you can?' Vera asked eagerly.

'I'm going to have a good try. Remember that we know what this creature from Procyon can do to the human race as time passes, and that we've got to stop him at all costs. Secondly, I resent being thought a fool. I'm no scientist, maybe, but I have a certain amount of intelligence, believe it or not. My aim is to be rid of Carter and Oena and be left holding all the valuable secrets. That way I'll be acclaimed as a great scientist — which ought to please you, Vera — and the newspapers who've been demanding I give my knowledge to the world will be satisfied. Once I'm rid of Carter I'll 'retire' from scientific activity, then I'll never be called upon to explain any of my efforts. Good, isn't it?'

'If it works,' Vera answered dubiously.

To this Harvey did not comment, but there was a tightening about his jaw, which seemed to indicate that he was quite sure of himself. In fact a rather surprising change had come over Harvey with the realization that he was the kingpin in the whole scheme. He was firmly determined to turn the tables on the ruthless alien who had so far pushed him around exactly as he had chosen.

The interview with Dr. Hargraves was a

long one, Vera and Peters staying in the car whilst it was in progress. When at length, two hours later, Harvey reappeared he was looking jubilant.

'Everything's all right!' he exclaimed, clambering back into position before the steering wheel. 'Hargraves got a flock of experts to work and there's no doubt that both formulae Carter gave me are the real thing. Each one is surprisingly simple and direct. The upshot is that Hargraves thinks I'm the greatest genius of all time. Tonight's papers will be full of my astounding prowess, and that added to my success with the levitator will certainly be something. I have thrown enough now into the lap of science to retire for good and rest on my laurels.'

'But what about your scheme for being rid of Carter?' Vera asked anxiously. 'That surely is the most important thing? If we don't get rid of Carter all the scientific 'discoveries' you have made won't mean a thing.'

'As to that,' Harvey replied, 'I've asked Hargraves to put into immediate construction a small space projectile, exact to the design and specification in the plans I gave him. I'm financing the prototype myself, and his picked team of engineers and experts will do the rest. He believes I want it for demonstration purposes, but you and I know better.'

'How long before it will be built?' Peters asked quickly.

'About two or three weeks I should think. Nothing very complicated about it. It uses magnetic lines of force for its motive power, rather like the levitator but in a different way. It's completely different from our present liquid fuel rocket systems, and only a fraction of their cost — otherwise I could never have afforded to have the prototype built myself. But once let me land Carter and Oena in a machine like that and Bob's your uncle.'

'I still can't see how it applies,' Vera said, puzzled. 'Surely Carter will be able to bring the projectile back to Earth, no matter how far away he gets in the first instance? After all, he's the designer of it!'

'He can, yes, providing the equipment doesn't die on him.' Harvey was grinning a little. 'I've had the whole thing over with Hargraves. He doesn't know what I'm driving at, mind you, and believes I am trying to determine how to prevent the mishaps that could maroon a spaceman in the void. What I am planning to do, on the strength of what he told me, is create a mishap, which Carter, for all his vaunted brains, won't be able to overcome. However, more of that later. I've got to think it out, and we need lunch. Then back to the lion's den for the operation!'

★   ★   ★

As Harvey had anticipated, the evening papers were full of praises for the scientific discoveries he had placed at the disposal of the public, through the agency of Dr. Hargraves, of course. It was considered even more wonderful that he — Harvey — asked no financial recompense for his efforts. The truth of this was, he just had not the impudence, for one thing, and for another he had quite as much money as he could ever use.

Besides, since he was making no financial demands he could refuse to see reporters and thereby avoid getting himself tangled up with things he did not remotely understand.

When he, Vera, and Peters arrived back in Buckinghamshire it was late evening. Dinner was eaten as usual, and there did not appear to be any signs of Carter having prowled around in the interval. Then towards nine o'clock Harvey made up his mind to take the plunge.

'And you won't let me come with you?' Vera asked anxiously. 'Honest, Harvey, I'm scared! I'm still afraid that he might kill you.'

'The gin-drinking mastermind goes out to meet his fate!'

With that remark, Harvey turned and left the drawing room, nearly colliding with Peters in the hall.

'If I may say so, sir,' Peters said, smiling awkwardly, 'I am deeply concerned for the risk you are about to take. If you would like me to somehow stand guard — '

'Only over my wife whilst I'm away,

Peters. Incidentally I suppose you've given Carter dinner. What mood is he in?'

'The same as usual, sir. Inscrutable.'

Harvey shrugged and went on his way. He found Carter in the lounge, apparently deep in thought. At Harvey's entrance he looked up. The room was warm, Harvey noticed, though no fire was burning.

'I fitted up my radiant heat system whilst you, your wife, and Peters were away,' Carter explained, reading Harvey's thoughts. 'And I gather from your thoughts that you are now satisfied that I did not in any way try to deceive you with bogus formulae?'

'Quite satisfied. You'll have heard over the radio and tv that the world thinks I'm the greatest benefactor ever.'

'I did not listen to the news: I prefer to brood when I am not actually working. However, I take it you are ready for the operation to be performed?'

'Quite ready. How long shall I be convalescing?'

Carter laughed shortly. 'Convalescence is an admission of poor medical skill, my friend. An hour after the operation you will be normal again. I have spent some little time preparing the basement for the job. Shall we go?'

Harvey nodded. 'Incidentally, how is Oena going on?'

'She is still in the ventilated steel cupboard into which you directed her. The circumstances of her creation were such that she will not require food or water for at least two days. She will of course be released long before then. At all costs I must preserve her.'

Since Harvey had nothing to say Carter led the way out of the lounge and to the basement stairs. Once he had descended them Harvey beheld for himself the change in setup. A long instrument table had been converted for surgical use and beside it stood a smaller table, its top littered with coldly glittering scissors, blades, and needles.

'Lovely!' Harvey commented. 'Just the thing to make the patient feel thoroughly cheerful.'

Carter shrugged and then motioned to the table. Harvey went to it and lay down, his head fitting into a specially made stainless steel headrest. Obviously Dr. Carter had been extremely busy making the necessary modifications to his weird laboratory.

'I hope you realize how much faith I am putting in you,' Harvey said, as Carter arranged his instruments. 'You can very easily kill me, but somehow I don't think you will.'

'Correct,' Carter assented, turning the knob on the anaesthetic cylinder. 'That way would defeat my own ends. Now, if you are ready?'

The anaesthetic cone descended over Harvey's face and he made no effort to prevent himself fading out. It seemed almost immediately that he was awake again, feeling very little different. He looked about him. Carter was wrapping up a long length of bandaging.

'Something go wrong?' Harvey asked, struggling into a sitting position.

'Why should it?' Carter gave him a glance. 'The operation was quite success-ful. You are fit enough now to move around if you wish.'

Harvey lowered himself from the table, marvelling at the alien's surgical skill in that he could so quickly destroy all weakening after-effects.

'Now,' Carter said, turning to the tall steel cupboard in which Oena was incarcerated. 'We will see what kind of a result we get.'

He unlocked the door and Harvey beheld the synthetic woman seated upon a stool within.

'Order her to come to you, Mr. Bradman,' Carter requested.

Harvey did so. In response the woman looked at him fixedly with her fascinating smoke-blue eyes. She seemed to hesitate over a thought, but she certainly made no effort to obey the order.

'Excellent,' Carter murmured, rubbing his hands gently together. 'Your brain now repulses her, Mr. Bradman. You are so to speak holding her at arm's length. All we require now is the adjustment to her brain so that she will respond to, and obey me. Since she is not controlled by either of us she may prove a little difficult.'

Carter turned aside and picked up a

bottle of bright yellow fluid. He tipped some of it quickly onto a pad and then made a sudden right turn so that he came quickly behind Oena as she slowly got on her feet and, for the first time, seemed to be taking an interest in the proceedings. With the pad pressed over her mouth and nostrils, however, she stood no chance. In a matter of seconds she began to sag weakly.

Immediately Carter caught her in his strong arms and took her to the table Harvey had vacated. What happened after that was such a masterpiece of brain surgery Harvey could only watch in fascinated amazement. Carter trepanned smoothly, even removing a section of the synthetic skullbone and laying bare the brain convolutions beneath. What he did then Harvey could not tell — some kind of ganglia adjustment presumably — but at length the skullbone was normal again and the air reeked of powerful antiseptics.

Harvey sat down and waited. Carter finished washing his hands and lounged around thoughtfully; then at last Oena began to stir and murmured something inaudible. Gradually consciousness returned to her and she sat up. Harvey had the instinctive desire to help her, until he remembered she was not a woman in the accepted sense. So he remained where he was, watching — as did Carter — the woman's movements as she slowly got down from the table to the floor.

'Oena look at me!' Carter commanded, and she obeyed.

'You are my creator,' she said haltingly. 'You made me. You moulded every — '

'Yes, yes, we know that. Sit down on that chair.'

Oena obeyed again, glancing straight through Harvey in the process. He might never have existed for all the notice she took.

'Everything is satisfactory,' Carter announced. 'From here on I can handle the situation for myself. I will see to it that Oena does not trespass on your territory, Mr. Bradman, and you will see to it that you do not trespass on mine!'

'That's a bargain.' Harvey got to his feet. 'I assume you mean to remain here indefinitely?'

'I do. With all my equipment here it would be foolish to do anything else.'

Harvey said no more. He left the basement and returned to his own quarters, to soon find himself almost overwhelmed by a joyous Vera and a politely relieved Peters.

'The man's a magician!' Vera exclaimed. 'There isn't the slightest trace of where he's operated.'

'No,' Harvey agreed, thinking. 'The job's done and he's down there with that synthetic woman. That's how the situation will have to remain until I get news of that spaceship of mine.'

A sudden thought of consternation seemed to strike Peters.

Hurrying to the bureau he scribbled a note and handed it over. Harvey took it and read:

IS IT NOT POSSIBLE THAT CARTER HEARD YOUR REMARK ABOUT YOUR SPACESHIP?

Harvey smiled a little and wrote back:

VERY POSSIBLE. BUT HE CAN'T POSSIBLY TIE THAT UP WITH IT MEANING DANGER FOR HIM.

'I understand, sir,' Peters said in relief, setting fire to the two notes and throwing the ashes in the metal waste bin.

Nonetheless it was difficult for Harvey — and in a lesser degree for Vera and Peters — to control their impatience as day after day passed and nothing seemed to happen. Peters, the only contact with the mysterious Carter, reported that he appeared the same as ever when meals were served to him, but on no occasion had there been any sign of Oena. Presumably she was in the basement.

During this uneasy period Harvey announced to the press his intention of retiring from science — which he did. To relieve the monotony he and Vera spent a good deal of time in London, following very closely their original pattern of life. Not that Vera any longer raised objections. Harvey, even though it had been by a fluke, had made himself eminent, and he had also shown that he was not lacking in courage.

Then, nearly six weeks after the brain operation, Dr. Hargraves sent word that the spaceship was completed. Where was it to be demonstrated?

'On my own estate here,' Harvey answered, over the telephone. 'Plenty of room in the grounds and it suits my purposes.'

'Right,' Hargraves responded. 'And do you want me to gather all the big noises of the scientific profession?'

'Later, yes — but not to commence with. I've a few tests to make for myself first, doctor. Have the machine delivered as soon as possible.'

'It will arrive this afternoon about three,' Hargraves promised. 'Travelling under its own power, of course.'

'Good enough.' Harvey rang off and then looked at Vera with a gleam in his eyes. To the rear Peters was hovering expectantly until Harvey caught sight of him.

'I — er — forgive me, sir, but I knew it was Dr. Hargraves and naturally I — '

'Of course, Peters. You're in on this as much as anybody. We'd better inspect the grounds and choose the best place for a take-off. I aim to try and reach the moon first. Come along outside.

'I added that bit about a lunar trip to throw Carter off the scent if he happened to be listening. It will seem quite logical to him that I should wish to try space travel now I have the machine to do it with. However, this is my actual plan, so listen carefully.

'When that spaceship arrives my first job will be to remove certain parts of the power plant. Hargraves himself pointed them out as danger-spots. With them removed the machine will start off all right, and will probably keep going for a clear sixty million miles or so — or even further in free space since no power is used except for take-offs and repulsion from a nearby body. Briefly, it means the vessel will take off perfectly, then it will cruise in free space with the power cut off: but the moment the power is switched on again the plant won't take the load. You can guess what will happen.'

'Two things,' Peters said. 'It will either crash into the nearest body or float through space until something stops it, retaining its original acceleration-velocity.'

'Good,' Harvey approved. 'You're quite

a scientist, Peters.'

'Sounds all right,' Vera said. 'But won't that kill off Carter? I thought you were against murdering him.'

'It won't kill him off because the machine is fitted with rocket jet recoils in case of emergency. He'll have enough power to make a safe landing somewhere, on another world maybe, but he will not have any chance of getting back here — unless he can create machine-tools out of thin air and remake the parts of the power-plant which are missing. That's a risk we'll have to take.'

'And why does he board the space machine without smelling a rat?' Vera demanded.

'Because Oena has gone aboard it and he values her too much to let her escape him. It's all a matter of timing. Oena has to be grabbed somehow and put in the spaceship. The spaceship controls have to be set by the automatic release, which will set the vessel flying into space at a certain time. And when that certain time has arrived, Carter has got to be aboard the vessel as well. I've got it all worked out.

When the machine arrives I'll do what I have to do to the power plant and pre-set the controls, then I'm going into Carter's quarters to tell him that I'm going to attempt a lunar journey and would like some advice — anything will do to keep him occupied. I'll tackle him in the lounge, and if he isn't there to begin with I'll get him there somehow. You, Peters, will watch for the right moment and then get Oena. By any means you care to adopt force her into that space machine. When that's done you, Vee, will burst in upon Carter and me and say that Oena has escaped and taken Peters with her — that should get Carter on the move, not to save Peters but to save Oena. By that time, Peters, you will have tied up Oena in the machine somehow and made yourself scarce. The instant Carter is in the machine we slam the airlock on him and clamp over the exterior bolts, which I have had specially fitted. The controls will work and — ' Harvey spread his hands expressively. 'I'm allowing fifteen minutes for the whole act.'

'I would remark, sir, that that synthetic

woman is stronger than I am,' Peters remarked. 'I might not be able to handle her.'

'There's some bright yellow liquid in a bottle in the basement,' Harvey answered. 'A square bottle on a little table. Put some of that on a pad and Oena will go out like a light. That's simple enough, isn't it? And you, Vee? You know your part?'

'In fact you have it all arranged nicely?' asked Dr. Carter calmly.

The three twirled round. They had been so absorbed in their planning they had forgotten everything else, forgotten even to keep their voices down. Carter was only a few feet away, an automatic in his hand. Beside him stood the queenly, superbly lovely Oena. 'All very ingenious,' Carter smiled. 'I overheard your remark in the lounge about a lunar trip, Mr. Bradman, and it was my intention to suggest to you a good position for your take-off. Yet I come out here to help, and what do I find — or rather hear? A deliberate plot to be rid of Oena and myself. It might even have worked — but not now. With a scheme like that you have broken your part of the bargain and I feel quite justified in killing you. By the way, this is not an ordinary automatic. It's a volatizer, capable of reducing each one of you to liquid flame.'

Harvey looked about him desperately, Vera clinging to him. He backed a few paces, Vera and Peters keeping time. Carter remained where he was, Oena smiling gently at him.

'Back out all you like,' Carter chuckled. 'I have a range of half a mile with this little toy. I like to see you scared — you miserable, cocksure little Earth people — '

He paused and glanced upwards as something almost transparent flashed through the sky from the south. It darted round and then began to circle over the estate.

'Ah, the spaceship!' Carter exclaimed. 'Your engineers seem to have made quite a good job of it, Mr. Bradman. I think I'll take a look at it before disposing of you.'

He watched the machine intently, and so did Harvey, Vera, and Peters. The extreme danger of the moment was forgotten by the three as the wonder-vessel darted back and forth and then finally settled into a steep downward drop.

'Something wrong!' Harvey yelled, grabbing Vera. 'Out of the way! He's going to crash!'

Stumbling and tripping, holding Vera's arm, he bolted for safety. Peters coming up behind. The scream of the uncontrolled machine flashing to earth was deafening — then it suddenly stopped and instead came the roar of safety under-jets. A blinding cloud of white-hot flame and gases smote the grass and carved an incinerating line. In the midst of it Carter screamed in anguish and Oena smiled gently as her body swiftly liquified and then exploded in a commotion of steam.

With a resounding impact the space-ship hit the ground and the din and confusion ceased. Acrid smoke drifted through the air.

'What — what happened?' Vera asked, shaken.

Harvey only shook his head dumbly

and Peters wiped the perspiration from his face.

Then the air lock opened and the tall figure of Dr. Hargraves appeared. He looked about him and then stumbled across the grass to where the trio stood.

'My dear Bradman, can you ever forgive me?' He grasped Harvey's hands. 'Of all the damned bad piloting that ever was! I lost control over the magnetic lines and the thing just fell like a stone. I'd have smashed up completely if the emergency rocket under-jets hadn't worked so well. Look at the machine! One side of her's badly dented. I should have employed a trained pilot, but as I hold a flying license myself I wanted to be the first man to use your revolutionary system . . . You must let the Association pay for the damage.'

Harvey fought for control. 'Small wonder you pancaked in a machine so unorthodox as that, doctor,' he smiled. 'As for the damage, that can soon be rectified.'

Hargraves drew the back of his hand over his moist forehead.

'That's all right then. Thanks for being

so generous. I wanted to make a nice easy landing and instead I nearly killed myself. In fact I would have done but for the sprung interior — ' He paused, frowning a little and looking about him. 'Just you three here?'

'That's right,' Harvey confirmed, tight-lipped.

'Mmm — just goes to show how the exhaust gas can diffract the light waves. I thought I saw five people for a moment as I crashed downwards.'

Harvey smiled and clapped him on the shoulder. 'You need a drink, doctor. In fact we all do; then we'll see about putting the machine right.'

Hargraves nodded, wiping his face with his handkerchief. As he accompanied the three into the house he did not notice, as they did, the blackened ashes that lay where the under-jets had gouged the earth. Dr. Carter of Procyon, and his ineffably lovely bride from the test-tube, had gone — forever.

We do hope that you have enjoyed reading this large print book.

Did you know that all of our titles are available for purchase?

We publish a wide range of high quality large print books including:
Romances, Mysteries, Classics
General Fiction
Non Fiction and Westerns

Special interest titles available in large print are:
The Little Oxford Dictionary
Music Book, Song Book
Hymn Book, Service Book

Also available from us courtesy of Oxford University Press:
Young Readers' Dictionary
(large print edition)
Young Readers' Thesaurus
(large print edition)

For further information or a free brochure, please contact us at:
Ulverscroft Large Print Books Ltd.,
The Green, Bradgate Road, Anstey,
Leicester, LE7 7FU, England.
Tel: (00 44) **0116 236 4325**
Fax: (00 44) **0116 234 0205**

THE ARDAGH EMERALDS

John Hall

England in the 1890s. The world of Victoria and the Empire. This is the world, too, of AJ Raffles, man about town, who, assisted by his inept assistant Bunny Manders, is a successful jewel thief. The eight stories in this book recapture the spirit of the Naughty Nineties, when the gentleman burglar would put out his Sullivan cigarette, don a black mask, outwit a villain, and save a lady in distress — and all before going out to dinner!

NO PLACE TO BE A COP

Frederick Nolan

The place is Manhattan, in the year 1878. A million people live in her teeming streets. She's a bitch. She boasts 6000 professional criminals, 5000 whores, and only 2000 policemen and twenty-eight detectives to investigate all the crimes committed. The New York Police Department deals with them all — from street-gang vendettas to sex murders and con men. And they also run up against a new phenomenon — a secret society called the Mafia in the district known as Little Italy . . .